The Goblin Child

and other stories

Michael Forester

Pegasus House Publishing

PEGASUS
HOUSE

First Published in Great Britain in 2016

By Pegasus House Publishing

www.michaelforester.co.uk

ISBN: 978-0-9955248-0-4

Cover Design by BookBeaver

Cover Image © Michael Forester

By the same author

Dragonsong

If It Wasn't For That Dog

These books can be purchased at Michael Forester's website:
michaelforester.co.uk

To subscribe to the mailing list email
michaelforesterauthor@gmail.com

The Goblin Child

by

Michael Forester

Published by Pegasus House Publishing

The matador on his knees, the dead bull his baby;
and the priest staring from the window
like a caged bear

I will only tell you
this: I have lived in both their temples,
believing all and nothing – perhaps, now, they will
die in mine.

Charles Bukowski, *the priest and the matador*

Contents

Acknowledgements

The Power Giver first appeared under the title 'The Change' in the inaugural collection of completelynovel.com
The Secret of the Perfect Vegetarian Risotto for One first appeared in the same collection.
Angel's Place won the 'Writing can be murder' prize at the Winchester Writer's Festival, 2009
Counting Eyes first appeared in the August 2016 edition of the Lakeview International Journal of Literature and Arts

1   Birthday

I remember my birth; the cosseted comforts in the sanctity of the silent darkness; the rising outwards, the feeling of intrigue in ignorant fascination.

Then germinated the anticipation of the severing of the We; the disquieting awareness that the Greater would expunge the Lesser, that the Stronger would banish the Weaker from the Eden of comfort for some uncomprehended sin. And as my I became Self and her She became Other, we felt the Lesser-that-is-I squeezed down upon by the Greater-that-was-One and driven into the tunnel.

"Reach for the light," said the muffled voice in whose crevices We had cradled Our Oneness all the days of Knowing. "Move towards the light," came the un-spoken words of Sentience that we had trusted beyond question as the spasm squeezed the Lesser to compel, to expel, to repel as never before. And the Lesser that was coalescing into the I struck out as instructed for the light that purported to welcome Us.

But oh, the horror when the I beheld the consequence of that fateful decision; when the I felt the pain of what we later learned to call "cold" upon the top of what we knew not was 'head' and the rough 'hands' that the I knew not were hands, that drew the Me out and away to the cold, cold, ice cold light.

There had been no resistance in the communion of oneness, for the Greater had always nurtured the Lesser. Then came fear and terror and squirming and pain as the coagulating I thrust in the panic of knowledge out from the centre in a premature attempt to give voice to the primordial scream.

And the scream was silent as screams are always silent when the ecstasy of the here-always-heart is burst by the never-ending dark-light swirl of the new-now.

And the screams were long and were ceaseless as it is right for screams to be, as the dark-light cold-hot dry-raw air screeched and scraped against that which had known only the caress of the warm gentle waters swirling about the I.

And the screams were, and the Greater was not.

And the screams were, and the Lesser was the I of the Me.

And darkness was upon the face of the deep.

"Push," came the sound from unknownness.

"Push," retorted the harshsome, fearsome, loathsome Greater, as its flesh compressed around the legs of the Lesser who knew not they were 'legs' in one final mighty thrust, expelling the Me forward and away, out of Eden's ignorance into the unending pain of Knowledge, the knowledge of the Greater's otherness and the inexplicable hatred of the I that was Me. For what else but hatred could cause the One with whom I was One to excise the Me from the We as so much discarded, redundant otherness?

The I was a repugnant odious bundle, expunged from the warm dark wanted place, more flushed than birthed, a dump of piss and puss.

Then at last came the words of final judgement of unending banishment and eternal excommunication, spoken by the unknownness over the not-waters of the cold, hard air.

"It's a boy."

2   The Goblin Child

If I really, really stretch my arms out I can touch the walls on both sides of the stairs. When Davey-at-playgroup reaches his arms out it's cos he wants to be a pretend airplane but I think that's silly. Davey-at-playgroup is a boy an' boys are silly an' I don't like boys I like girls better cos girls are much more growed up than boys. An' when I stretch my arms out I know I'm nearly growed up cos when I came to Nanna-gran'dad's house the last time an' stretched out my arms I couldn't reach the walls only the wooden rails stuck on the walls so that's how I know I'm big. I asked Daddy when that was an' he said that was nearly six months ago an' that's a long time an' I'm a much bigger girl now than I was then an' I'm nearly growed up.

Daddy drove me here in the car yesterday an' I sat in the front an' Daddy said I could cos now I'm a big girl an' Mummy didn't come. But he said I had to not ask 'when will we get there?' an' 'how long will it take?' cos big girls don't do that an' Daddy said I would knowed when we were half way cos we would stop at the café where all the lorries stop an' he would have tea and I would have orange squash and then we would both do wee-wee in the little toilet out the back with the funny door with writing on it an' then it would only be an hour 'til we got to Nanna-gran'dad's house. I don't like to do a wee-wee there cos the toilet smells funny an' there's always water an' toilet paper on the floor an' I asked Daddy why an' he said it was cos there were some very mucky people in the world but it would be alright if I didn't touch anything an' I didn't touch anything an' it was alright.

An' when we were in the car again I asked Daddy why Mummy wasn't coming to see Nanna-grandad an' he said she was tired an' she needed a rest an' could I be a big brave girl and stay at Nanna-grandad's house for a few days with just Nanna-grandad and not with Mummy and not with Daddy? An' I said "'Ummmmmmmmmmm" an' Daddy said not to do one of my 'ums' just now cos this was important an' he could ask me to be brave and growed up because now I'm big. An' I said "Yes." An' then I asked if Nanna would still make gingerbread houses with me even though I was nearly growed up an' Daddy said "Yes," an' I asked if Gran'dad would still read to me from the big story book an' he said he would. An' I asked why did Mummy need a rest an' Daddy said it was cos she was tired an' I asked why was she tired an' Daddy said "Cos mummies always get tired when they make baby brothers and sisters" an' I said "Is the baby going to have blond hair and blue eyes?" cos I heard Mummy say it would cos then it would look like Daddy an' then he said "Look!" an' we was passing Mr. Rodhay's farm which is five minutes from Nanna-gran'dad's house an' there was a tractor an' cows an' sheep an' I waved to the sheep but not to the cows cos I like sheep better than cows. An' Daddy said Gran'dad would prob'ly take me to see the sheep an' Mrs. Rodhay would most prob'ly give me milk from the milking an' an apple scone an' then we was there an' I'd been a big growed up girl an' not asked 'How many miles?' or 'How long will it take?' even once.

Nanna made us tea an' I had jelly but I didn't eat the bits of fruit in the jelly. An' granddad said what a big girl I was and how much I'd growed up since he last saw me an' I said "Please will you read to me from the big story book when I'm in bed before you go to work?" an' Gran'dad said "Of course I will Jenny-Wren" an' I said "Don't call me Jenny-Wren, Gran'dad, cos I don't like it." An' when it was bed time I went to put my pyjamas on. An' when Daddy came to tuck me in I asked "When are you going home an' when are you coming to get me?" and he said he would be gone when I woked up tomorrow but he would come to get me in a week an' I said "How long is a week?" an' he said "It's seven tomorrows," an' I showed him I knew how many that was on my fingers. An' then Gran'dad came to read me from the big story book an' he asked did I want a new story or an old story an' I said I wanted a new story an' he read me a story an' it was called 'The Goblin Child.'

Went to the doctor's today. Nothing wrong really... nothing hurting... no symptoms. Just wanted someone to listen to me. I feel so fuckin' crap all the time. Not been to work in a week. Manager keeps phoning but I let the answer phone take it. Duplicitous bitch sounded sympathetic at the beginning of the week. It was all 'Are you ok?' and 'We do understand that you're expecting a baby,' and 'We want to do everything we can to support you.' By the end of the week it was 'Where are you Ms Thomas? It is essential you return my call. We need a certificate immediately or we may have to take this matter further.' So I saw the doc. Couldn't tell him anything – there's nothing to tell. Except that I'm a worthless piece of shit and I don't deserve to live and I don't deserve a healthy baby so I know it's gonna be sick or it'll be mongoloid or hydroceph or have no head at all. Because that's what I deserve. Worthless fuckin' bitch. Not good enough to live let alone bear a beautiful child. But you can't say that to the doctor, can you? So I just told him I was feeling a bit off colour and he handed me a two week sick note without even looking at me. Another two faced sod who doesn't give a damn. But why should he? I'm nothing.

When I wake up crying I know I'll be crying all day. At first I'd ring Tony at work and snivel down the phone at him. He rushed home the first time, thinking there's something really wrong. But when he got here and I just went on crying he got frustrated. Then it was all "Sweetheart, I came out of an important meeting because I thought you were ill. I thought something awful had happened. I thought you'd lost the baby." 'Course, that's what I deserve. I'm gonna be a shitty mother if this kid ever gets born. Don't know if I want it any more. So now I keep my tears to myself and Tony thinks I'm fine. At least he can pretend he thinks I'm fine and concentrate on his fuckin' job. So let him. I'll just sit here and maybe I'll even shit here. Not washed in three days. Disgusting, isn't it? But then that's what I am – disgusting and worthless. Too exhausted from doing nothing to do anything. Just sit here with the TV on and the phone pulled out of the socket. The friggin' sick note's still under the hall table where I dropped it last week.

An' it was called 'The Goblin Child,' an' it was about a beautiful Queen in a land far away. An' she was sad cos she couldn't have a baby and the King was sad too cos there would be no one to be King after him. Then one day an old woman in a shawl came to the palace and said she would make the Queen so she was having a baby, but the King had to give her anything she wanted if she did an' King said "Yes" an' the woman made the Queen so she was having a baby. An' when you're having a baby it takes a long time cos it's taking Mummy a long time. An' when the Queen had her baby borned it was a beautiful little boy with blue eyes an' blond hair an' the Queen was so happy an' she bathed him an' played with him an' loved him an' I'm going to bath Mummy's baby an' play with him an' show him my toys but he won't want to play with my dollies cos boys don't like dollies. An' the King was so happy an' everyone in the palace was so happy. But a week after that the old woman in the shawl came back an' said to the King that he had promised her anything she wanted. An' the King said "Yes" an' the woman took off her shawl an' she wasn't an old woman but she was a goblin woman with a long hairy nose with great big warts an' she was really, really ugly. An' from inside her shawl she took out a goblin baby an' everyone in the palace gasped which means they made a funny noise cos the goblin child was so ugly an' it was so ugly you couldn't tell whether it was a goblin boy or a goblin girl. An' the goblin woman said "Give me your baby and I'll give you mine." An' the King said "No!" an' the Queen said "Nooo!" an' everyone in the palace said "Nooooooooo!" But the goblin woman said "A promise is a promise an' you have to." An' it was just like when Maisey promised to lend me her Camille Ballerina with the tutu an' didn't want to but Mrs. Jones said she had to cos she promised so she did. An' the goblin woman took the beautiful baby boy with blue eyes an' blond hair an' gave the queen the goblin baby instead an' everyone in the palace cried.

Tony says I need help; that this isn't normal. He says he knows women are supposed to have postnatal depression but I've not even had the baby yet. Says it's abnormal to cry so much. I say, "So you try being twenty-five fucking weeks pregnant *Sweetheart*, and see how you get on with sixteen weeks of vomiting followed by four months of carrying a friggin' beach ball round in your stomach. Then we'll see how normal you'd feel and maybe you'd wanna bawl your fuckin' eyes out too." Christ only knows why he's still here. I don't want the bastard anymore and I don't want any more of his fuckin' frogspawn in me either. He makes me sick with his stroking and fawning over me. I know what he's after. Just wants to get his dick up me again. Well that's how I got this lil' bundle of joy in the first place. So the bugger can just go wank over Playmate of the Month for now. It's what he deserves for turning me into breeding stock. Christ only knows why he'd wanna fuck me now anyway, the state I'm in... He's a good man really. I'm the problem. I deserve to die. And I want this fuckin' frogspawn to die.

He made the appointment for me. Drove me there. Walked me into the surgery with his arm hooked through mine, as if he was frightened I'd run away. Sat with me in the waiting room to make sure I went in. Can't blame him. He'd coped with me 'til I phoned him up in his meeting in Aberdeen on Wednesday. He was pissed off at me for interrupting him and said we couldn't go on like this. Then I screamed down the phone at him that I was on the balcony and I was going to jump. Christ, his tone changed then. Fourth friggin' floor we're on. That would have made a mess. Mummy and frogspawn squished all over the pavement. Must have got someone to phone the police while he kept me talking... telling me he loved me... telling me that everything would be ok. Coppers arrived while I was on the phone... blue lights... neighbours twitching curtains... nosey parkers lined up on the pavement outside... the works. They broke down the door while I was still on the phone... not talking... just crying... crying so hard... can't stop crying. So here we are at the shrink's ready for sentence to be passed. I'll take what's coming... won't be that bad... they don't execute women for being thirty-two weeks pregnant.

It's the wrong fuckin' drug! Here look at this web site I've found – and I quote: "Fluoxetine can cause risks during pregnancy, both to you and your baby. All women have a 3% to 5% chance of having a baby with a birth defect. If you are taking Fluoxetine during the third trimester your baby may experience complications." Fuckin'

Prozac. Should never have been prescribed it. And now I'm gonna have a spastic baby. From frogspawn to retard in six easy weeks. He's taken my baby. Not even born yet and he's taken it... changed it for... an aberration... a monstrosity.

An' the goblin woman disappeared with the baby boy with blue eyes an' blond hair an' everyone in the palace was sad an' the Queen was most saddest of all. An' the Queen said to the King, "Why did you give my baby away? You have to get him back." So the King asked this Wizard "What should I do?" an' the Wizard said the Queen had to take the goblin baby deep into the forest an' leave it there an' not look back an' if she did everything would be alright cos when she got back to the palace her baby boy would be back but if she looked back it wouldn't be alright. So the Queen said "OK" an' took the goblin baby into the forest an' it was dark and she was very frighted.

That incompetent sod gave me the wrong fuckin' medicine. And now there's water on the floor and Tony's drivin' me to the hospital and I can't stop it! I can't stop it! I can't fucking stop the goblin child!

An' the goblin baby was frighted too, an' it was cryin'.

Home a week. I don't wanna look at it and I don't wanna touch it. Greedy little sod's on my friggin' nipple the whole time and I've got nothing left to give and I'm crying the whole time and Tony's going berserk sayin' if he doesn't get back to work the company's gonna fold and I'm saying "Well get the fuck out of here then and leave me to this soddin' goblin rat" and he's saying "Wadda you mean goblin? He's beautiful – blue eyes and blond hair – looks exactly like your brother... he's beautiful Jen, can't you see how beautiful?" An' I'm saying no, he's deformed. Can't you see? He's a fuckin' goblin child. I hate him an' I want my baby back... give me back my fuckin' baby!

An' the Queen put the baby down on the ground all wrapped up like this... an' the forest was dark an' scary an' the Queen was really, really frighted. But she left the goblin baby like she was told only when she turned away the baby cried an' she thought it sounded like her baby so she thought the goblin woman had brought her beautiful baby boy with blue eyes back an' she turned around.

She turned around. She fuckin' turned around. Don't you see? My baby's a goblin cos the queen turned around! It's taken thirty years but the friggin' queen turned around and I'll never get my baby back!

But when she turned around she saw the goblin baby was still there, only it just sounded like her baby an' then she was even more frighted cos she remembered the Wizard had said she shouldn't turn around or everything wouldn't be alright. An' she was so frighted she ran an' she ran an' she ran like when I race Maisey home from playgroup until she got to the palace. An' when she got to the palace everyone was laughin' an' dancin' an' singin' an' the King was holding a baby. An' the Queen thought "Oh! My baby comed home anyway an' it's alright after all," only when she looked at the baby it was still a goblin baby. But the King said "No, it's our baby, can't you see it's our beautiful boy with blue eyes an' you can bath him an' play with him again." But the Queen could see it was a goblin baby even when everyone else in the palace couldn't see it an' she died of a broken heart.

I'm calmer now. I'm rational. You can back off. Everything's safe. I'm completely in control. Everything's gonna be ok. I've worked it out now. I know what I have to do. An' this is one fuckin' Queen who won't look back.

3   Sometimes They Don't Come Back

There's a full moon tonight, and a sky full of stars, but they're hidden behind a dense bank of cloud. He's waited close to the drop point, concealed behind a tree since before 23.00 hours with nothing to read but the Flight Plan – or FP as everyone calls it. Transport was running ahead of schedule this evening; a bureaucratic foul up by some secretarial pen pusher who was too busy filing her nails to concentrate on the less consequential matter of Field Operative safety. Net result: two hours waiting here until entry time. 'Do Not Pass Go. Do Not Collect Two 'Effin Hundred Pounds,' he thinks. He watches the second hand on the face of the clock on Tesco's fancy tower. On the dot of 01.00 hours he snaps his fingers. The lights wink out one by one in perfect sequence all the way down the street, just as if there'd been a real power cut. 'At least Environment got their timing right,' he thinks. He drops the night vision goggles over his eyes and the world lights up again – for him, at least. Checking his equipment one last time, he moves over to the house – a Victorian halls-adjoining semi. Immediately he sets to, examining the Poppies (that's Possible Points of Entry if you're a rookie). The alarm flashes disdainfully at him. He'll wipe the superior smile off the bugger's face in a few moments. Electro-mechanical security's a doddle. Windows? Screw-locked: too noisy to undo; door? Dead-locked, bolted and chained. Pas de probleme.

He draws his Obsidian from its sheath and touches its point to the lock. He waits for the familiar clicks as the latch complies with the instruction, the bolt draws back and the chain drops loose. One finger to the door is enough to make it swing back fractionally. He's small; doesn't need much room to get through. He takes his last breath of unpolluted air, crosses the physical threshold of the house and simultaneously crosses that invisible boundary between honesty and dishonesty; goodness and turpitude; his world and theirs. He stands in the hall – if standing's the right word for someone who hovers six inches above the floor (he loathes the Queen's new Imperial measurements and refuses to use them, even in official communication; Cubits and Palms were good enough for his grandfather's grandfather and they're good enough for him). The faint buzz from the pack on his back reassures him he has more than enough flight time to complete the assignment. Finally he is forced to exhale and takes his first breath of foul air. His stomach retches and he fights to control the urge to vomit. He glances to the left through the lounge door. A glass topped coffee table covered with weekly magazines and coffee mugs, torn envelopes and pens, the lid from a tub of strawberry Ben & Jerry's, wet side down on the red leather sofa. The infrared on the TV reminds no one at all of the machine's state of readiness; all the detritus of everyday human existence and nothing whatsoever that makes him want to be part of it.

He checks his FP again. He can't remember the last time he's made a mistake, but he checks anyway. 'There are old pilots and there are bold pilots,' as the old mess hall cliché goes, 'but there are no old, bold pilots.' Almost noiselessly he glides forward over the tiled floor, ingrained with dirt transferred from six generations of footwear, until he reaches the stairs and begins the upward phase of the journey. The pitch of his motors rises with the effort of gaining the necessary height.

Research has already warned him in a carefully worded email about the Feline. They'd become very specific about recording their advice last March, when an Operative had been lost. Research had claimed they'd advised of the presence of a PAE (or Potentially Aggressive Entity as the bureaucratic style of the Ops Manual put it). Operations swore blind they'd not been told. It didn't really matter who was lying. The Field Operative never came back. Everyone had become more careful after that – careful in practice and more careful still in box-ticking, triple-carbon-copying back-covering.

He's over half way up the stairs when he sees it on the landing. A full sized tabby, standing maybe two thirds of a cubit at the shoulder. Its back is stiff and arched, its fur bristling. It spits and snarls venomously. How can something he's never seen before hate him so much, he wonders? He hovers, draws the Obsidian wand from its sheath again and waits for the creature to make its move. The problem isn't that it will harm him, no matter how evil the filthy creature's intentions towards him. It's that if he kills it, it will probably scream. He's learned over the years that freeze-framing's a better option. But that takes real skill. You don't get two chances. As he anticipated, it leaps at him from the top stair, legs straight out, claws fully extended, mouth twisted into a howling grimace of unadulterated hatred. He returns no aggression – he's long since understood that emotion makes him less efficient. In a perfectly timed response, he dematerialises momentarily, then re-materialises and twists round just in time to see it close its paws over the place he had just been occupying. Without hesitation he flicks the wand down hard. He's gauged the energy level perfectly. The creature stops in mid-air just above the fourth step from the hall floor, level with a picture of a lighthouse hanging slightly askew on the embossed wallpaper. He continues to hold the wand steady until he's sure the animal's frozen, then lowers it carefully in the direction of the hall floor. Its body hesitates for a moment, then follows the trajectory that the wand has described, coming to rest silently at the foot of the stairs. It will wake there sometime later during the night. The whole operation has taken a little over three seconds – time allowed for in the FP, but time he would prefer not to have expended.

He waits a moment to reassure himself that the household is still sleeping, then turns his attention back to his ascent. Just before the top of the stairs he dons his oxygen mask (probably unnecessary at this altitude, but standard procedure for all structures above ground level, and anyway, it helps a bit with the smell) and continues to the landing. Four doors, all closed. He consults his FP again. Straight in front, bathroom (*'no relevance'*) . Next to it, adult bedroom (*'avoid entry'*). Next to that, airing cupboard (*'heat source – extreme danger of death'*). And finally, children's bedroom (*'Target: Female, four years'*). He returns the FP to its case and checks again for sounds of wakefulness anywhere in the house. Then he proceeds to the children's bedroom, points the wand at the handle and blows on it until it swings gently back. He hovers in the doorway, peering through the night sight.

Two beds. Not bunks – at right angles to each other against the wall. Thomas the Tank Engine printed on one quilt, Barbie on the other. A shelf lined with books. A Paddington Bear boot perched on top of the tower of a plastic castle; two Action Men, limbs entwined in a faintly obscene pattern; Postman Pat and an over-stuffed teddy surveying it all non-judgementally from the window ledge. He enters the room. The human stench is more powerful now, the oxygen mask not helping much. Human pups have a far stronger scent than the full-growns. It's evolution's way of ensuring the parents can detect them at a distance. As instructed by the FP, he heads for the Barbie bed; sees the target; hesitates. The operation disgusts him, however many times he repeats it. However often he laughs with the other Field Operatives in the mess hall after the missions are over, it's still sickening, soul-blackening work. He might as well be a cess pit cleaner.

At the bed he descends towards the sleeping child. Her body is covered by blankets. Only her head is showing, long blond hair cascading over the pillow. However often he does this, they still disgust him, these kids – warm-blooded, elephantine and swathed in far too much flesh. Always, always they seem to sleep with their mouths open. He has no alternative but to fly straight through the path of her breath. He tries to time it so that she's breathing in as he does, but he can't avoid the out-breath when he lands on the pillow. He gets giddy with nausea. But he's a pro and he's learned to control it; all but the stomach retching that is – that's pure reflex action.

And now follows the act of defilement that has long since cost him his soul. Of course, he'll laugh about it with the rest of the squadron when he gets back; pretend he finds it funny no matter how loudly the last vestiges of his conscience scream at him. He steadies his breathing, bends all four knees 'til he's crouching. Latex gloves will give him some relief from the impact of handling human flesh. Latex; one of the few human inventions for which he acknowledges gratitude. With both hands he reaches under the pillow; finds the fuel nugget immediately – a large, nicely rounded piece. He knows by the feel of it in his hands that it will transmogrify perfectly. He tugs gently. The child stirs but does not wake. Mercifully she rolls over, turning her face away from him. With the removal of the pressure of her head the enamel ore comes away easily and he glides quietly backwards with it in his arms and down to the carpet. He rises again, drawing the compensation from his back pack. Christ, what a fuckin' euphemism. What kind of compensation do they call this? A coin of the realm. One pound sterling for an enamel nugget that will keep a full sized thaumaturgic generator operating for a week. OK, so it's Treasury's responsibility to set the exchange rate – mid-nineteenth century, one groat, mid-twentieth, sixpence, now, one pound. But even after all these years, even after so many, many transactions, he still finds it hard to reconcile himself to the fundamental unfairness of the exchange. He suffocates his whimpering morality and draws the coin from his pack; unfolds it; rises to the bed, holding it in front of him like an enormous tray and carefully slides it under the pillow. He is momentarily confused as it clicks against something hard. And then he understands; realises that he is now confronted with the crowning glory of his career: that fabled moment whose very existence is disputed daily over endless jars of nectar in the mess halls of every airfield in the land. This is it; the fabled *Double Exchange*. In the whole of his career he's never met a single Operative who actually claims to have made a double exchange. He doesn't think anyone really believes they ever happen. He's overcome with excitement; shaking; can barely control himself. He has to steady his hands to reach round behind the coin and fix his grasp on the second fuel nugget. Now he draws it around the coin and once again balances it carefully as he lowers himself to the floor. He stands back, shaking his head in disbelief at the scale of the evening's transaction. He is overwhelmed by a surge of guilt, for he has no further coin to exchange for the second tooth. But his conscience is all but dead and the guilt is rapidly displaced by the thought that the Operation Plan contained no reference to there being a second nugget. Of course it didn't. How would the Department know? The computer programmes make no allowance for statistical aberrations. He knows already that he will not report it. The second fuel nugget is his, and it's going to make him fabulously wealthy.

But now he sees the problem; how to carry two nuggets when his pack is designed for one. Quickly he decides and places the first nugget into the pack. The weight is considerable, but he is not daunted. He will carry the second in his arms and will conceal it somewhere near the Extraction Point before Transport arrives. When he's certain he remains undiscovered, he will return and will break it down to sell piece by piece on the black market. He can't even begin to get his head around its value.

He bends all four knees again, leans forwards and lifts. The effort is phenomenal. Mentally he instructs the motors of his gossamers to lift him. Their pitch rises until they are screeching, but the weight is too great and he remains floor-bound. Eventually he gives up, reconciles himself to the fact that he will have to drag the second nugget, cubit by cubit across the floor and down the stairs. He looks around for something to serve as a harness. He sees what he needs on the bed and sets the nugget down in order to rise and pluck a single strand of golden hair from the target's head. As he tugs on the strand, the follicle snaps out of the skull without warning and slaps across his face. It's enough to disturb the target. Though she does not wake, she turns again and he's subjected to a full-frontal blast of her breath that sends him spinning backwards with both the airflow and the stench. Still he clings onto the hair, spinning out of control, downwards to the carpet. He hits it with more force than he should; much more force. He's concerned the crash landing will have damaged his gossamers. But no matter now. Dazed, he picks himself up, checks his Obsidian is undamaged, then places it carefully inside his flight jacket – Q Division will have his hide if he brings back any more broken wands. Satisfied as to its safety, he winds the hair several times around the fuel nugget, binding it firmly. He then twists the other end repeatedly around his own body and across his gossamer wings, rendering them inoperable even if they are undamaged. But no matter. They are useless to him now anyway.

He checks the knots one last time to ensure the nugget is indeed bound firmly to his body.

He turns towards the open door.

It is then that he sees the cat.

4   The Pretty One

In the summer of my ninth year you returned, your wanderlust not abated, merely suspended. Air kisses flew like smoke rings through pursed crimson lips while hugs, stiff as long dead corpses, silently attested to our family feuds. Then twilight fell, the ten o'clock shadows shimmering empty glasses through the heat haze and adult voices, tired of supressing aphorisms to preserve my prepubescent innocence, insistently demanded my withdrawal.

Across the chamomile lawn you called, sending me to bed, but not empty-handed. Fearful, I held back, lest your presence evaporate with the night.

"Look what I have for you."

My hand, still seaweed-stained from solitary beach games reached out to you for… something I did not have the vocabulary to articulate. The gift you proffered, a purse, woven by hand upon the shores of Tahiti, you said. It could not pierce those armoured stains and lay passive, friendless upon my upturned palm.

Later, under the safety of soft sheets and solitude, I opened it by torchlight to find two hairgrips, orange and green, and a note that said '*to hold back your fair hair, my pretty one.*'

I peer back across lost years, incredulous that you thought me old enough for such sarcastic gestures, knowing then and now what it was you really wanted me to hold back.

The hairgrips are gone, handed on to the two daughters I fathered years after your death. I still have the purse. Its woven strands of vermillion, turquoise and magenta can pierce my armour now. Inside it I keep my memories of you, extracting them only in the safety of solitude. I will never set them free, neither these, nor the certainty that you left because I was not the like-for-like replacement you wanted for the black-haired girl-child you had aborted.

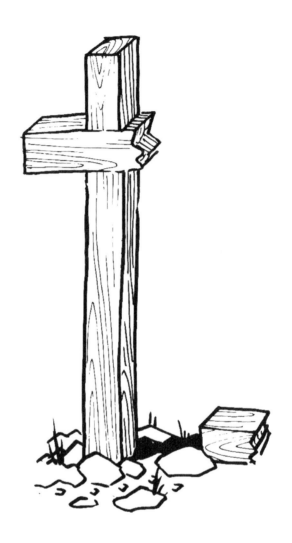

5   For Show and Tell

For show and tell this week Miss said we had to bring our gods to school. On Monday morning we lined up outside the classroom, everybody holding tight onto the hand of their god. It's easy to lose a god if you're not careful, you know. The gods were well behaved. Well, mostly.

Inside the classroom, Miss said to leave the gods in the corner by the coats. I'm afraid they got into a bit of a muddle, so that at show and tell time some of the kids couldn't find their own god. Then there were arguments over whose god was whose. Some of the kids started crying and others were fighting. Ali and Mary had grabbed the same god. They both said it was theirs and no one else's and they pulled so hard it broke. They ended up with half each and now they won't speak to each other. I suppose a bit of a god is better than no god at all, but I think it would be better to share the god. Gods like being shared and they work much better when their children allow them to be whole.

James said it didn't matter, cos his god was the only one that was real anyway. That made Ambar cry and throw hers away. She said she didn't want a god unless it was real. Later, when she stopped crying, she realised James was wrong and her god had been real after all. She went to look for her but I don't think she's found her again yet.

When my turn came to talk about my god, I was a bit shy. You see, he's a very old god. He was my dad's when he was a kid and his dad's too. He's really worn from being cuddled and loved so much. I don't care though, because he's a very wise god and I tell him all my troubles in bed at night. Sometimes I wonder if he's nearly worn out, he can take so long to answer me.

6   Angel's Place

It was the hands he noticed first – big and bony, out of proportion to the rest of the body. Angel had seen it all before, of course, seen them stride in, full of bravado and bluff, then later limp out, deflated and depleted, licking their wounds emotionally and physically, sore from the bruises and sore in the soul.

He slid his eyes slowly up and down the delicious young creature that stood in the doorway to the bar. The daylight filtered in from the street behind the boy, silhouetting him. A weak light bulb just inside the door was little competition, throwing a muddy yellow half-light onto the face and body. But even in that light Angel could see that in years to come the skinny, lanky frame would fill out and the boy, already six feet tall, would be muscular and broad shouldered. But not yet. For now he was all gangly limbs and beating heart, trying so hard to look grown up.

Angel continued to watch, faintly amused, as the boy stepped forward and the door swung closed silently behind him. The kid stood, blinking for a moment, waiting for his eyes to adjust to the lower light level. He hesitated, taking in the scene around him – irregularly scattered tables and chairs, some occupied by couples, their limbs knotted tightly around each other; uneven hardwood floorboards, strewn randomly with sawdust; a juke box mumbling incoherently in the corner and a long c-shaped bar, repeatedly varnished in some dark wood stain, sticky with the residue from the bases of untold numbers of glasses.

He maintained his position in the corner behind the bar, corkscrewing a towel into a beer glass that was already dry, waiting for the kid to make his move. Now that the light had evened, he was able to reassess the quality of the merchandise. The first impression of height and build was right, but now he could make out facial features – dark, almost black eyes, an olive skin that hinted of Mediterranean origins, an oval shaped face let down only by cauliflower ears that had never been pinned back. Not a big problem though – for young limbs and a strong, energetic body, many of his regular customers would pay well.

The kid began to move uncertainly, easing his way slowly towards the bar, as if trying not to look out of place. "Green as a new mown lawn," sighed Angel to himself. Putting down the towel and the glass, he strolled casually down the length of the bar, running his right index finger through the thin film of grease on its surface as he approached the spot where the boy had stopped. He slowed, standing directly in front of him, only seventy centimetres of wooden surface between the two of them, the upturned bottles on their optics reflecting in the mirror behind. Angel looked up from his own five foot four height into the boy's face. The blond highlights in the black hair, the imitation gold medallion round his neck, the chain about his waist, were all carefully assembled in an attempt to create an image of confidence and power. Yet they did nothing to conceal the insecurity that heaved insistently up and down inside his chest, a cork on a sea of turbulence behind his controlled exterior.

For a moment Angel and the boy stood holding each other's gaze, arm wrestling with their eyes. Finally Angel spoke. "What can I get you?"

The kid was silent for a moment. A slight motion around the shoulders betrayed the fact that he was considering turning and running. Before he answered, a low voice, Glaswegian accent thick as hot tar, drawled lazily from a dark alcove to the right of the door. "Whatever the laddie wants, put it on my tab, Angel."

"Sure thing, Jamie," Angel replied without taking his eyes from the boy who had still not spoken.

The exchange seemed to shake the kid out of his trance. He faltered a moment, shook his head slightly as if becoming conscious of where he was for the first time. He looked nervously around himself at the room and the customers, and then back at Angel. He dropped his eyes and began to turn. "I'm in the wrong place," he mumbled almost inaudibly. "I have to go." The kid turned to re-trace the twenty feet back to the door, gathering pace as he approached it.

He almost made it out to the safety of the street, too. But at the moment he leaned forward for the door handle a leg shot out in front of him and connected with his calf. The boy stumbled and twisted, collapsing forward, while his shoulder struck the doorframe with a sharp crack that reminded Angel of a wooden plank snapping. Angel winced as if feeling the pain himself. In a moment the boy was on the floor – kicking his arms and legs about him in confusion like a helpless, upturned beetle.

"Now, now, laddie." It was the same dark voice that had spoken before. "Don't be in such a rush to go. We haven't even begun to become acquainted yet." Angel watched with his usual disconnected sense of the inevitable. The boy, still dazed, put his hand on a chair, dragged himself to his knees, then lifted his face towards the man who had addressed him from the darkness. Wordlessly, he stood, pulled back the chair and slid down into it, rubbing his shoulder where it had struck the doorframe. On his face his expression slowly changed. Anger…resentment… uncertainty… respect… and was that adoration? Angel sighed, shook his head slightly and went back to drying beer glasses. Breaking the kid in had taken Jamie even less time than usual.

"Now," drawled the molasses-coated voice from the shadow of the alcove. "What'll it be, laddie?" The boy squinted into the semi-darkness, still nursing his shoulder and mumbled an unintelligible reply. "Louder, laddie!" snapped the voice from the darkness, rolling the 'r' so that it sounded like a Gatling gun. "I asked you a question. What do you want to drink?"

The kid looked up fearfully. Then hesitantly said, "You say, Jamie. You say what I want to drink."

"Ahh," replied the voice from the darkness, "you're learning independent thought. That's good. I like a laddie who knows his own mind." Then in the direction of the bar, "Bring me another Glenlivet, Angel, and a Knockout for the laddie."

Throughout the exchange Angel had been standing with his back to the bar, continuing to towel the already dry glasses and adjusting the optics. At the mention of the drink he stiffened. In the mirror, an almost imperceptible ripple shuddered across his jaw line and disappeared, virtually too quickly to notice. "The boy's young, Jamie. Take it easy." Angel delivered the response without turning.

Immediately there was a sound in the alcove of a chair being scraped sharply back across the floor. Then a half empty beer bottle flew out from the darkness in the direction of the bar, turning end over end, spewing beer as it flew. It smashed against a Bacardi bottle upended on its optic, and fell just short of the mirror behind. Angel leapt back in shock as the shards of both bottles sprayed indiscriminately over the wall and the floor and the bar. Then he stood motionless facing the mirror. The room, already silent but for the whimpering of the juke box, seemed to grow still quieter, the air charged static with anticipation. Angel did not need to turn to know that every eye in the room was upon him.

The voice that followed the bottle out of the darkness was even and measured, without emotion. "Angel that will be two glasses, one for the Glenlivet and one for the Knockout. That's Absinthe, French Vermouth, Gin, and a *lot* of Crème de Menthe. You do remember how to make it the way I like it, don't you, Angel?"

Angel had little time to compose himself. He considered not replying but knew Jamie would take silence as further provocation. Picking one of the more obvious pieces of glass from the folded cuff of his shirt sleeve he responded, "Yes, Jamie, I remember." His voice carried the mixed tones of suppressed anger and suppressed fear. His hands shook visibly as he placed onto the tray the five bottles, a whiskey glass and a pint glass, the latter filled half full with ice. Then he carried the tray around the bar, stepping as carefully around the glass on the floor as if he were executing long memorised ballet steps, and walked towards the darkness.

Reaching the table in the alcove, Angel lowered the tray slowly onto the ring stained table and turned to walk away. He had almost arrived back at the bar, his back still to the room, when Jamie spoke again. "Pour them." Angel knew the instruction was not intended for the boy. The shudder across his shoulders and the back of his neck were more easily visible this time. Without a word he returned to the table and stood motionless, feeling the suspense and the fear and the elation and the glee as the impromptu audience looked on from the tables around the room, eager for confrontation, hungry for blood. He swallowed hard.

Dark patches began to appear around the armpits of his white t-shirt.

"Do you really need me to tell you twice, Angel?" The voice carried theatrical surprise but remained even. The speed of delivery was still easy, almost nonchalant. "You know what happens when I have to tell you twice."

Angel hesitated, considering his options. Then a whisper. "Yes, Jamie." Hesitantly, he reached for the Vermouth and slowly unscrewed the cap. He had tipped it to the edge of the boy's beer glass and was about to pour when Jamie spoke again, very slowly. "Wrong order." The voice was a drop forge now, still Gatling the 'r's and stamping each word down into Angel's ears, resonating with his nightmares. "You remember what happens when you get the order wrong, don't you, Angel?"

Angel's hand shook violently, the shudder passing up through the vermouth bottle to the beer glass, tipping it slightly from the table. The kid reached forward to stop the glass from falling. "Did I ask you to do that, Laddie?" The question was snapped; rhetorical. The boy's hand snapped back as if burned. "What happens when you get the order wrong, Angel?"

Angel shook silently for a moment, unable to speak. The bottle continued to vibrate, though now he had managed to lift it fractionally from the rim of the beer glass. Refraining from answering was not an option. A whispered reply; "You... come."

There was a moment's silence. "Where do I come to, Angel?"

"You come into... Angel's Place."

"Very good, Angel." Jamie's voice was overtly condescending now. "I come into Angel's Place, don't I? And do you like it when I come into Angel's Place?"

The response came slowly, inaudible to all but Jamie and the boy. "No, Jamie. I do not like it when you come into Angel's Place."

"You do remember when you were seven, don't you, Angel?"

A silence.

"Yes." The response was a whisper once again, but the rising panic was clearly audible.

"You do remember what I gave you for your birthday when you were seven, don't you, Angel?"

Angel was weeping now, his chest tight, his breath coming short and hard.

"Yes, Jamie."

"Then many happy returns, Angel. Many happy returns for seven. And how could we forget eight and nine? Many happy returns for eight, Angel. And many happy returns for nine. And many happy returns all the way up. So pour in the right order, Angel. And don't let me have to tell you again."

Angel returned the Vermouth to the tray and picked up the Absinthe, his hand still shaking uncontrollably. Steadying his right wrist with his left hand, he poured a double measure of the green liquid into the beer glass and returned the bottle to the tray.

"Very good, Angel. Now let's see if you can get the rest of it right, shall we?"

Angel was barely aware of a pleading look from the kid as he picked up the Vermouth bottle once more and slowly unscrewed the cap. The tears still streamed down his face. Despite his shaking hand he matched the measure of Absinthe with the same quantity of Vermouth. Jamie remained silent as Angel reached for the Gin. Angel could feel his eyes though, fixed unswervingly upon him as they always had done, every time he had performed the ritual. Finally, and with a steadier hand now, he reached for the Crème de Menthe. From this bottle, too, he poured an equal measure, tipping it back as the required level was reached in the glass. He had returned the cap to the bottle and the bottle to the tray when Jamie's voice came again.

"Keep pouring." The words were clipped, delivered very slowly.

There was the sound of a sharp intake of breath as Angel drew in his stomach muscles, then simply stopped breathing.

"Keep pouring or... *I... will... come.*" There was menace in the words now.

Barely suppressing a reflex action to vomit, Angel re-opened the Crème de Menthe bottle. There was a slight clink, as glass touched glass, and he continued to pour, the mixture turning darker green in the glass as the liquid neared the top. Angel returned the bottle to the tray and exhaled deeply.

"What are you waiting for, laddie?" There was no uncertainty over who Jamie was talking to or what he intended. The boy looked helplessly at Angel. Then a swift glance over his shoulder told him all he needed to know about the sneers and smirks behind him. He turned back to the table and looked into the semi darkness of the alcove. He opened his mouth to speak.

"Drink it." The drop forge hammered down again, driving the instruction deep in to the boy's terror. "Drink it all down." The tone was still condescending menace. "Then I've got a lovely sticky lollipop for you under the table." A ripple of semi-suppressed giggling passed round the room like brushwood catching fire.

The boy reached an unsteady hand for the glass. His fingers closed around it and he raised it to his lips. He sipped, grimaced. "There's a good laddie. Keep drinking." The tone became menacing again. The boy continued to sip the green liquid. Jamie started to sing softly under his breath. "Happy birthday to you." The 'r's' rolled again, tumbling over and over each other, as the Glaswegian accent poured, like melted chocolate onto the floor.

The whole of Angel's body was shaking now. "Happy birthday to you." He put his hands to the table to steady himself. "Happy birthday, dear Laddie." He gripped the edge of the table mercilessly, the skin on his knuckles and the back of his hands turning white with the pressure. "Happy birthday to *me*."

As the boy continued drinking and the angle of the glass began to level in front of his mouth, a sound came from Angel's throat. First a soft moan. Then a louder groan, audible to Jamie and the boy. Then louder so that the audience could hear. Finally Angel opened his mouth and roared, "No!"

The voice from the darkness began to speak again. Something about Angel's Place. "Remember Angel's Place," that was it.

Angel's grip on the table did not falter. It was momentarily unclear as to whether or not the movement was voluntary, but his arms lifted, and with them the table. However it started, in a moment the act had become deliberate, and Angel upended it onto the voice in the darkness. Jamie's chair fell backwards and the table came down on top of him, the only part of him protruding from underneath, his face; on top of the table, Angel. The kid saw his moment. The mixture hadn't taken hold yet, and in a second he was up and out through the door. Gone.

Angel's weight had Jamie pinned to the floor. He reached out with arms and legs to maintain his balance as Jamie thrashed unsuccessfully underneath to free himself. By chance or by design, Angel's hand found the Absinthe bottle. It was intact. Holding onto a table leg with one hand to gain stability, he brought the bottle to his mouth and drew out the cork with his teeth. For a moment it was unclear if he intended to drink. But then he upended it, and in a single determined movement forced it down into Jamie's mouth. He was screaming uncontrollably now, but still intelligible.

"This is for seven Jamie. Remember seven? Happy birthday Jamie. And for eight and for nine. And all the way up, Jamie. Happy fucking birthday from Angel."

7   The Shoe Wearers

Legends passed from mouth to ear in secret congregation in the night, tell of times when Great Ones walked our land.

Erect and proud they strode, the stories say, bearing spears of bravery through endless summer grasslands of the sun. How fair this land that sired my nation; the rich, red land; here where our fathers' fathers' fathers laid their once-wise, twice-blessed bones to stir the dust that made the children yet to come.

Then to our land came Shoe Wearers. Speaking of a god that died for love, you came. "Shod with the Gospel of Peace," you said. "How happy are the feet upon the mountains of him that brings good news," you said. "Our god will wash your feet," you said.

"Who is this god who washes feet?" we asked. "And why must feet be washed of good red soil?" We who revered the lion's roar and claw knew not the northern bear that hugged, and crushed, and stole the breath of life from those that strode too confident upon the land.

You were they who washed the Master's feet, you said. Now you have mastered us and it is only right that we wash yours, you say. We wash them with our tears and dry them with our hair, my brothers say; not for guilt as ones you caught in sin, but in our own repentance; bitter, sad repentance that ever we sat by to watch you inch your feet into our yards and shoehorn us from wealth to slipshod poverty. My brothers call you jackboot looters. You stamped your heels into the faces of the Generations, they say.

Yet I cannot believe that this is so, for you have brought us 'Progress.' Look! We are shod to walk the roads you said we needed. And I am truly grateful for the shoes your people send – though I know that they do not make me a Shoe Wearer in my heart.

And so it is, I wonder.

Shoe Wearers, can you tell me this: why, in these shoes, can I not feel the heartbeat of our land? With all the learning you possess that I know makes you more than we can ever be, please tell me this.

Why are we sore where once we soared?

And why are we raw when once we roared?

And are the rumours true? Was there, long ago, a fire that once burned incandescent in our soles?

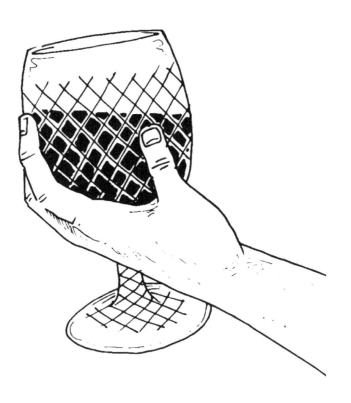

8   Summer's Over

It's over.

Summer, I mean. But so is the relationship that we have known, and life is never going to be the same again. They tell me I'm clever with words, so I'm using my words now to try to express how I feel about your going. How many different ways are there to say it: separation; break-up; leaving; divorce; ending. Maybe now that you've gone I'll write them out, calligraphy style, just like you used to do. Then I can stick our life together in a scrapbook. At least I'll have the memories.

Of course, you will say that none of those words is appropriate. It's merely a matter of life taking its natural course. Some things have to end so that others can begin. You say you'll go on loving me even now that you've gone. And maybe in a way that is true. But I know full well that when you have readjusted, orientated yourself to flying solo, one night across a crowded room some other man is going to catch your eye and sweep you off your feet. I am powerless to prevent that now.

Eighteen years is such a long time. I don't know how I will carry on without you.

Last night you packed your bags. This morning you carried them downstairs. That's something else that's different now. You used to let me do that for you. It's yet another change that marks the passage of time and the evolution, the entropy of our relationship towards its inevitable conclusion.

So now, I am seated at the table across from where you used to sit, where I looked into your eyes. Eighteen years you sat there. Now all I have to look at is the Beaune Premier Cru which I swirl around my glass. The cut of the crystal catches the sunlight through the wine, making ruby fairies dance across the ceiling. Their swirling chaos celebration of sensuality transports me back across the years.

I remember the day we met, or rather the night. The snow was still piled up on the street corners. Only those that had to, ventured out that night and neither of us had any business being away from the warm places we had just left. But you were insistent that we were to meet for the first time.

Strangely enough, when faced with the reality of a real confrontation after months of expectation, your confidence left you. You could not speak. Your companions had to make a point of introducing you to me. You were so damn shy that I don't think you had a word to say for yourself all that evening. But it was your eyes that got me. I'll always remember your eyes. I was smitten. People say there is no such thing as love at first sight. I know different.

Of course, on your side, it took a little longer to develop. But pretty soon you'd moved in with me and I knew deep inside that this relationship would last a lifetime. Mind you, there were times when I wondered whether we were going to make it. The first few years were tumultuous. So little articulate conversation passed between us, and so much screaming characterised our early relationship. Mostly yours – but I did my share of shouting too. Sometimes you seemed incapable of responding to rational persuasion. We both matured a little as the years rolled by, didn't we, Sweetheart?

We'd been together maybe four years when you asked me to marry you. Was it a leap year? I can't remember. But I knew the question would come one day. I was prepared for it. I tried to explain to you that no matter how much I loved you, I could not do as you asked. For I was legally wed to another who would not release me. And that despite this, my heart was yours. I would live with you as long as you would stay with me. I don't think my answer ever really satisfied you. So perhaps even then, all those years ago, it was the beginning of the end. For, from that point forward, your attention seemed to focus beyond the boundaries of our relationship. I asked you not to change. You told me my request was impossible for you to fulfil. You were urgent to grow. I can't blame you. I had turned down your invitation to the altar. You needed to make whatever provision for yourself you considered fit.

It can only have been another year or so after that that you determined that an academic future would be yours. You bounded yourself about with the tools and trappings of book learning and I could feel you beginning to slip away from me. I could have fought it, I guess. But this was your route to personal growth and your tutors were so complimentary about your mental prowess and achievements. Who was I to hold back a superior creative power? I guess, looking back, the real surprise is that it has taken you so long to come to your final decision to leave.

How greatly I enjoyed observing the growth and increasing sophistication of your intellect. Does that sound patronising, Sweetheart? It really isn't meant to. I've always had the utmost respect for your cerebral capacity. And that's without reference to the overwhelming artistic capability that you have displayed throughout the time that I have known you. Where does it come from, Sweetheart? I know both your parents very well and neither of them shows anything like your capacity for artistic self-expression.

Your early works, those that you executed soon after coming to live with me, were in some ways the most impressive of all. Abstract in the extreme, I never understood what you were getting at in them. But I could tell from the intensity of the way you tackled the canvasses that these were no mere scrawls. Rather they were the work of a true artist whose talents had yet to reach their zenith. You painted life as you saw it then, a unique perspective to which I found it so hard to relate. I don't know if you remember, but you gave me some of those paintings. I kept them. I always will. They are a part of you I don't have to relinquish even now.

But as the years rolled by, your attention moved more to structure and form and your work took on a somewhat more integrated character. At last I could begin to relate to some of what you saw, some of what moved you.

It seemed to me that you reached your heights of expression in sculpture. There was so much of you in that final piece you created. I was desperate for you to give it to me. Do you understand why? You see, you had completed it at the beginning of the summer. And though you did not say, indeed, you even denied that you were leaving, I knew that the completion of that piece in some sense marked the end of your apprenticeship. And I knew from that moment you would be leaving. It simply took you a little longer to realise that you were actually going to go.

And now summer really is over and you've gone. The leaves are falling copiously outside. We used to shuffle through them hand in hand just for the pleasure of the sensation around our ankles and the crisp crackling that brought joy to our ears. I shall not do that with you anymore. Autumn's nearly over too. So many summers; so many autumns. Winter approaches.

I could have tried to stop you leaving. But what good would that have done? We had reached a congruent ending. And I, of all people, know how important it is for endings to be congruent. So how about we celebrate your departure by an exchange of gifts? Let me have the sculpture, Sweetheart. It marks our parting. This story is my gift in return.

So now here I am alone, opposite your empty chair watching the ruby fairies dance across the ceiling. They swirl and spin joyfully. They dance hand in hand, as if to mark your having come of age.

It isn't often a daughter leaves for University.

It isn't often that a father has to say goodbye.

Come back and see me when you can.

9　A Small Ration of Jumbled Egg with Prawn

Intent upon raising herself from the ashes to a life of glass slippers and ball gowns, Cinderella sweeps the dust of Walthamstow from her feet and boards the Stanstead Ryanair on a one way special to Torremolinos. Sleeping the flight away in her sardine sized seat, in her dreams Prince Charming is a muscular Latin lover astride a Harley Davidson, his mysterious eyes hidden by mirrored aviator Raybans. Two days later, reality finds her leaning against the outside wall of a sea front night club at 3.00 am on a cold Sunday. Here she squanders her virginity on a penniless timeshare tout who thrusts inside her to the rhythm of the bass drum, pausing periodically to upend a bottle of tequila.

She never goes home.

Now her crow's feet point to midnight and her coachmen have turned to rats. She drowses her days away in a cocaine-hazed studio basement eleven rows back from the sea front and works evenings in a poorly-lit tapas bar. Here, her diminutive Spanish boss, a slithering mollusc of a man, undresses her with lecherous eyes while attempting to translate the menu by way of a Spanish–English phrase book. Reflecting on her confused and equally ill-translated dreams, Cinderella finally acknowledges she has completed the transition to ugly stepsister. Sadly, she recounts the specials to Josh from Northampton and Eddie from Walsall. Reassuring herself that everyone outgrows childhood dreams, she inscribes on her pad yet another order for a small ration of jumbled egg with prawn.

10   Anatidae

In Camilla's opinion – and she is the first to acknowledge it is just a personal opinion – ducks don't get a very good press. They're either treated as the butt of everyone's humour (well would you want your species represented to the world by a speech-impeded bi-polar celluloid animation in a sailor suit?), considered insufferably fluffy and cute, or they end their lives on a plate in some ignominious restaurant. Camilla says – and I'm beginning to wonder if there mightn't be something in her opinion – that there's rather more to the species Anatidae than first meets the eye.

Camilla is one of those people who knew her purpose for being on the planet from an early age. Her babyhood was populated (her word not mine) with the likes of Jemima Puddle-duck and the Ugly Duckling not to mention the usual whole host of animated creations such as Daffy, Donald and so on. Her decision, at the age of fourteen and a half, she says, to become an unswerving Pescatarian was an instant one upon being presented with a Gordon-Ramsay-at-Claridge's Sunday lunch of duck in plum sauce. It was, she insists, an ethereal experience. The spirit of the duck on the plate rose up in front of her and delivered a stern lecture on the demerits of cutting short the lifespan of a fellow inhabitant of the planet, particularly one even less earthbound than oneself, at that. While her sixteen-year-old sister (her mother would have preferred a bigger gap between them but the family's Catholic origins have been traced back to well before the Protestant Reformation and her husband's attentions in the early years of their marriage were, to say the least, consistent), Ophelia, and her six-year-old brother Miles chewed their way contentedly through their respective allocations of similarly unfortunate anatidae, Camilla's feathered apparition simply denied her the capability of lifting her arms from her sides in order to facilitate the consumption of the portion of the Good Lord's bounty set before her. Mummy scolded her. "Camilla, if you do not desist forthwith from embarrassing me in front of all these *people*, I will never, *never*, bring you to London again."

Daddy coaxed her with, "Come on Cammy-kins, grown up girls *love* duck. We'll never make a deb of you if you don't learn to eat properly in public, Cammy-popps."

Her elder sister taunted her with, "This week duck conservation, next week tadpoles, no doubt," accompanied by her most cultivated withering look. Her little brother kicked her shin under the table. But none of this persecution moved Camilla. Her resolve was complete, her mind made up, her decision taken. From that moment forward Camilla Forthergil Hardington-Smythe was a convinced disdainer of meat (fish being tolerable since ducks eat it themselves), and an aspirant leading light of the International Duck Rights Movement.

After that weekend in town, the family returned to Gloucestershire and the Rectory. As the summer shadows grew longer, Sir Henry F H-S's attentions returned to his desk at the Ministry, his rather intriguing new copper-haired secretary and his two-nights-per-week unavoidable sleep-overs at the Dorchester. Lady Seraphina returned to her habitual twin preoccupations of the vicarage garden party and the Ladies' Bridge Circle. Camilla was left to while away her long school holiday in any way she pleased so long as it did not disturb her mother nor bring embarrassment to the family. This environment, combined with unlimited access to the internet provided, in short, a veritable incubator for the development of Camilla's socio-cultural transmogrification.

Camilla had established entirely to her own satisfaction that while eggs removed from Daddy's breeding pens might stand a lesser chance of hatching than if left under their mothers, such chicks as she did manage to hatch stood a considerably better chance of survival in her tender care than they would in the outside world upon the arrival of 1st September. Accordingly, she established a methodology for the covert removal of said eggs that she considered every bit as ingenious as the escape routes established through wartime Vichy France for the smuggling of downed British airmen out to neutral Spain. Her method was, in fact, brilliantly simple. Being as yet a little, well, underdeveloped, shall we say, she acquired and donned a bright red 34 inch C cup bra, waited around the pens until no one was looking then fill the underutilised cups of said item of attire with part-incubated eggs and made off with them without guilt or backward look.

Camilla's days were spent happily in the Rectory's hayloft providing supported incubation of a not inconsiderable number of future generations of duck, by means of the periodic application of her hairdryer. Sadly, the experiment was not entirely a success and to Camilla's profound disappointment by the end of the first week in August she had been able to hatch very few ducklings. Well, in fact, to be scrupulously honest, she had hatched none at all – but, as she was quick to point out, there were still some eggs undergoing her tender attentions and she was confident of achieving an eventual successful outcome.

During the same period, the nocturnal hours that other family members were wont to squander on unnecessary amounts of sleep, were devoted by Camilla to the development of her rationale, her underpinning philosophy, her 'Principa Platyrhychos,' as she was minded to think of it, by means of internet research. So diligent did her commitment to her vocation prove to be, it was inevitably not long before she found herself involved in regular blogging leading to frequent Facebook exchanges and culminating eventually in numerous Microsoft Messenger conversations with persons whom her mother might potentially have considered less than entirely suitable companions for her teenage daughter. But – and Camilla was entirely right about this, of course – this was the second decade of the twenty-first century, she was an exceptionally mature young woman for her age, and in this Brave New World (which unlike others she had actually read last term at Roedean), advanced Young Thinkers prioritised matters of fundamental principle above the parochial opinions of their parents, their parents' friends and the children of their parents' friends.

In retrospect, it was perhaps predictable that somewhere amongst the bloggers and Facebookers and Tweeters, Camilla would eventually encounter her nemesis. What the more ironic amongst Camilla's associates might perhaps have predicted was that said nemesis might be found in the form of an individual who utilised the online pseudonym, 'Duck.'

In her *Seventeen* diary the next day, Camilla wrote that she would remember the 13ᵗʰ August that year for the rest of her life. It was, she wrote, her coming of age, her rite of passage, the relinquishing of her spiritual virginity. (The perpetuation of her physical virginity was an irritant of which she really would have preferred to be rid and which required only the arising – in part literally – of a suitable opportunity. However, she did not consider any of the spotty, overgrown, post-pubic, emotionally-underdeveloped male *children* who had made clumsy advances towards her so far to constitute anything like her idea of a suitable opportunity. Of all the young men she had confronted in her now not inconsiderable span of years, the only one she could describe as different was Duck.

She had encountered him on the 'Vegans For The Protection of Endangered Wild-Fowl-Supporting Marshlands' blog. She had first been drawn to the demonstrable intensity of his commitment. What he lacked in variety of vocabulary he more than made up in vehemence of expression. And anyway, appropriately contextualised Anglo-Saxon aphorisms were perfectly acceptable methods of self-expression in this day and age, especially if one did not have the privilege of a long and exquisitely expensive education.

By means of further Internet searching she established Duck to be a twenty-five-year-old anarchist who earned his living as Junior Assistant to the Editor-in-Chief of the newly established London based publication, 'The Worker's Noble Sweat.' His press photo in *The Sweat* confirmed the appropriateness of his hair length and disdain for conditioner, the correct degree of wear in his jeans and the wholly reassuring hole in the top of his left Doc Martin boot.

Thereafter she had, unsurprisingly, gone out of her way to seek out the venerable Duck on Facebook. It took her little time to discover that he styled himself in a most original manner as an Animal Rights Revolutionary whose avowed intent was to replace the Government with an Action for Animals Soviet, outlaw private property, ban all forms of motor transport, give England back to the working classes and someday become a helicopter pilot

(Camilla considered the latter inconsistency too minor to be of relevance). As she read his Facebook manifesto, a strange warmth began to spread itself through her body, she was conscious of a hardening of certain parts of her torso that hitherto she had been taught were unmentionable and an almost melting feeling in other formerly equally unmentionable parts. Before she had finished reading she knew without question that this was the man to whom she was destined to give herself, to spend the rest of her life with, the man whose children she would bear (she rather liked the idea of three: two boys respectively called Sebastian and Calum and a girl for whom she had yet to determine a suitable nomination).

Engaging Duck in an online conversation was the next hurdle Camilla needed to leap. She was fully aware that while she considered herself to be a sophisticated adult in all but years, it did not necessarily follow that all others would automatically concur in this opinion. Accordingly, she determined to establish an online alter ego of her own. While her days were devoted to the careful nurturing of her soon-to-be-hatched dependants, at 9.00 pm precisely she would tear off her daylight persona and reveal herself as 'Muscovy', a twenty-one-year-old copper haired femme fatale, Protector of *The Environment*, Champion of All Water Fowl. The identity was complemented as a result of a few minutes' research on the internet by a 1997 picture of Danica Mae McKellar that she was quite certain would go unrecognised after all these years. She noted a mental addendum to ensure that she did not become too retro in her personal styling tastes as a result of this essential obfuscation.

The strategy was entirely successful. Within twenty-four hours she had engaged Duck in a preliminary conversation that left her, at 1.30 in the morning, in a state of sufficient arousal as to prevent her from achieving sleep, regardless of how many times she single-handedly addressed the root cause of her disturbance. As the sun rose over the barn she acknowledged her exquisite defeat and made her way out to the hayloft, comforting herself with the knowledge that Muscovy and Duck had arranged a further online tryst for 9.00 pm that night. Under other circumstances she might have taken as an inauspicious omen the fact that two of her six remaining eggs were a little cooler than she remembered them to have been the previous afternoon.

The second night's encounter led to the exchange of mobile phone numbers. Her mother had replaced her phone only that week when Camilla had announced she had mislaid the handset her father had given her for her fourteenth birthday. "Just promise me, darling," she had said, "that you won't tell Daddy – or at least not 'til you're due back at school. You know how upset he'd be at your carelessness."

Camilla had wanted to Skype but Duck indicated his dislike of the medium. No matter, a sufficient degree of intimacy could still be achieved with the exchange of short delayed texts and real time words on Messenger.

A total of some four days had passed from their first Messenger exchange when Duck declared himself to be in love and proposed they meet at Reading. By this time they had discovered a shared love not only of wetland water fowl but also of Eminem and Biffy Clyro, both of whom were headlining at the Festival. Duck had said a mate of his had given him press tickets, so they'd be able to get in no cost, no trouble.

Camilla was delirious with excitement. She had but six days before their proposed meeting on the first night of the Festival in which she had to plan the entire encounter in exquisite detail. There was also the minor impediment to be addressed of how she would explain her absence from the Rectory for upwards of seventy-two hours.

Her planning rapidly took on the resemblance of a military campaign, triple underlined and fully annotated within the pages of the 'Seventeen' diary. Her excuse for her proposed absence was easily established in the form of a fictitious sleepover at the home of Imogen Fitzhugh. She had determined never to speak to Imogen again after the incident last term involving the theft of Maxine de Beauchamp's unopened packet of feminine hygiene products for which she was quite certain Imogen was solely responsible. Nevertheless, Imogen's father's estate lay conveniently close to Reading and Imogen herself coincidentally happened to be looking for an excuse to meet her own boyfriend. They agreed, in the briefest of phone calls that ran only moments over two hours, on a common story that would sound plausible to all concerned should subsequent cross examination ensue.

Camilla's route and transport from Gloucestershire to Reading was straightforward. When her mother dropped her at Gloucester railway station she would simply wait for the red Mercedes SL to drive away, change into suitable travel/festival clothing (baggy t-shirt fastened under the breasts, torn off jeans, Doc Martin replicas constructed of manmade materials) and hitch her way down the M5 and onto the M4 along with all the other festival attendees. She was entirely confident of her ability to overcome the small matter of the dissimilarities between the photograph of the twenty-one-year-old Danica Mae McKellar and the physical presence of Camilla herself. There was also no question in her mind but that she would offer Duck her body on this, their first encounter, and she anticipated a night of bliss in the North Face Tadpole tent that he had already informed her he was bringing to the Festival.

There was but one remaining matter that troubled her. Giving Duck her body was no problem – quite the opposite. But Camilla felt the gift to be an insufficient expression of the true commitment of the inner person that she wished to make. She wanted Duck to know the totality of her devotion, that this was a once-and-for-life bonding. Only a gift representative of their shared commitment to matters pertaining to the *Survival of the Planet* would do. The only gift that would suffice was her remaining six duck eggs. She would transport them to Reading in the same manner as that in which she had liberated them from the breeding pens – in the cups of the red brazier. She would keep these tiny creatures, so helpless yet so important, warm and nurtured by her own body heat. She would pass them to Duck who would do the same. If necessary, she would permit him to don the red brazier to sustain the incubation. It would be as if they two were parents of these tiny saviours of Nature. This, and this alone, would represent to Muscovy and Duck the depth and intensity of the unbreakable commitment they were making to each other and to the planet.

Camilla's journey to Reading was less than wholly comfortable owing to the difficulty of keeping the eggs evenly against her chest to ensure they all received their fair share of her body heat. She ignored the suggestive looks from several male festival-goers hitching from the same roundabout as she reached down inside her bra to ensure the eggs were well settled. She even poked her tongue out at the one who had said "Want me to do that for you, Sweet'art?" Nevertheless, she remained deeply happy, joyful one might say, at the personal and planetary significance of her pilgrimage.

When she finally arrived at the main entrance, there stood Duck waiting for her, almost everything she had hoped for. She had to admit to herself that he looked, well, a little *older* than he'd said. Had she known better, had she been older herself and a better judge of age, she might well have put him nearer forty than twenty-five. Nevertheless, as he took her in his arms, kissing her long and deep, fumbling immediately under her t-shirt for her breasts, not once did he question her own age. And it was not that age gap that made Camilla realise the mistake she had made. It was not his evident experience in disrobing the female form he betrayed by his ability to unclasp her bra with one hand, nor even the fact that he dislodged the eggs in his fumbling attempt to grab her essentially non-existent breasts that made her revoke there and then her proposed commitment. Rather, as the eggs cascaded to the ground, some to be entirely destroyed and others merely cracked, it was his response to the demise of these precious lives that finally crystallised Camilla's decision.

Momentarily subdued, Duck looked down upon the scene of near genocidal devastation for which he alone was responsible. Then he looked up apologetically at Camilla.

"Aw, never mind, doll," said Duck, grinning, "we can scramble 'em instead of boiling 'em."

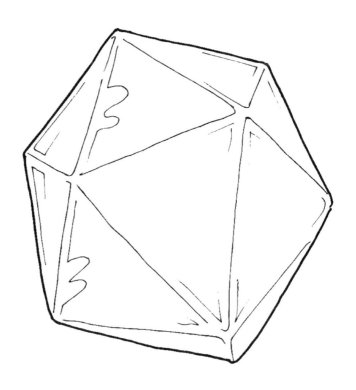

11   The Meta 4.0

Was it my parents who first determined that I should be a writer? Certainly they were both lovers and creators of literature. I will never know, of course, for the decisions that set our courses in life, the stars by which we later navigate, are placed in the firmament long before we ever begin to use them to set our sextants. It is only when we discover that the coastline we presumed to be the Indies is in fact the Americas that we realise we have been using unreliable guidance systems. All I can tell you – and this only because they later told me themselves – is that they started to teach me to read with flash cards when I was well under a year old. Their consistent attention over the months that followed resulted in my mastering the usual children's books – 'Mister Men', and the like – well before I started school. I will always remember their delight (my parents, that is, not the Mister Men) as they later recounted to anyone who would listen, each of the accomplishments they marked up on the ethereal honours board they faithfully maintained for me until long after the end of my childhood. I will be eternally grateful to them for this deeply planted and well-watered love of literature that I have since possessed throughout my life. Perhaps they will understand if I am less grateful for the pain that I still associate with the memory of their disapproval. This I earned on those occasions when I chose to play with friends or watch television in preference to reading or writing. For though their words repeatedly confirmed to me that the choice of how I spent my time was always mine, the withdrawal of their approval evidenced by their disinterest in any non-literary achievement that in my immaturity I might chose to value, was always too great for me to bear. I learned quickly to return to the loving parental embrace for which I hungered so deeply by the rededication of my time to literary endeavours. Eventually, as my absorption of these values became complete I presumed them to be my own. Thereafter it simply never occurred to me to make choices of which I knew by instinct they would disapprove. I have held ever since a disposition for accommodating their preferences above my own.

By the age of eight, the decision had already been taken that I was to be a writer. At eleven I had completed my first book of children's stories (unpublished, of course) which mother insisted, until I turned seventeen, that I should read in its entirety to all visiting relations and family friends. They, who would undoubtedly have preferred to discuss my father's prize-winning novels to my pathetic offerings, were thus condemned to suffer smilingly the purgatory of my earliest banalities. But on the other hand, I, an emotionally typical teenager, was forced repeatedly to undergo death by a thousand embarrassments each time I read this pathetic little volume out loud. At fourteen the middle school had performed my first play (I recall that my father's donations to the school's swimming pool fund were, coincidentally, surprisingly generous at around that time) and by eighteen I had been granted a place at Bath to study critical and creative writing (the selection tutor's first enquiry at my interview was after the health of my mother).

On admission, freed from direct parental control for up to ten weeks at a time and exposed to what passed as the cutting edge of literary thinking, I might easily have gone awry. Fortunately, my internalisation of the unyielding principles of right and wrong was long complete, my moral compass instinctive. My work I took most seriously; the drinking competitions in the bar, sporting prowess and sexual exploration of either kind (I had not established a preference at that stage), less so. My academic marks were exemplary and parental praise on visiting weekends was appropriately prolific. If I sensed a near undetectable unease from one or other of my parents over my leaning towards criticism rather than creativity in my selected courses of study, I, like they, was apt to dismiss this short-lived aberration as no more than temporary youthful flirtation. All three of us were confident I would, in due time, revert to the highest calling and commence poetic or prosaic composition in earnest.

When a First with Honours led to a Master's Degree (in creative writing, naturally) at the universally acknowledged best writing school in the land, it caused pleasure but no surprise to my parents, my mother merely inscribing yet another achievement in those amorphous gilt letters on the impalpable honours board. My future was now set. I would, without the slightest doubt, surround, storm and take hostage whichever glittering literary citadel I chose to possess and rule.

That, of course, was until I met Professor Anthony Cultt. Of my first piece of work Cultt was utterly dismissive. While the shock of this rejection by someone so clearly *in loco parentis* was, to say the least, profound, I redoubled my efforts and made further submissions. When dismissiveness transmogrified into comprehensive disdain I became seriously concerned. And when, on that final afternoon as I stood in front of a workshop of some thirty graduate students, he pronounced my efforts as being "devoid of any emotional integrity whatsoever", I was driven beyond my design capability. I at first swayed, but held my footing. As all looked on, almost imperceptibly, I began vibrating until it was evident to the assembled that I was shaking violently and uncontrollably. Then, like an over-tensioned bridge cable that had been required to hold up too much, I finally snapped. Whether, as it was later testified to the Disciplinary Committee by Professor Cultt, I had actually beaten him about the head with my fists while screaming, "You insensitive, egotistical bastard; you waste of a carbon footprint; you over-credited substitute for an emotionally intelligent entity," is actually immaterial. The fact of the matter is that I offered no defence and the committee thus found against me unanimously plus one (the Committee Chairperson specifically requiring it be recorded in the meeting that she cast her superfluous casting vote for the motion). I was dismissed and required to leave that afternoon.

As I read back over that last paragraph, I can all but hear you say that you find the anecdote uncharacteristic of me. Since I am, in your mind, merely a character in a story, it is essential that you find me convincing. Do you think I have claimed for myself excessive free-flowing eloquence, too lively a wit and too great a confidence, such that I exceed credibility? Sadly I fear it so. For though what I have written above is how I would have wished matters to have proceeded, my need to have you cast me as a reliable narrator requires that I admit the responses I claim above occurred only on those innumerable occasions on which I have relived the events. And yes, I must acknowledge that it is only because time and countless repetitions of the scene on the stage of my mind permit my re-scripting of the drama that I am able to cast myself in such heroic guise. The reality, of course, is that I slunk away, red-faced in embarrassment in front of a room full of my peers whose chief emotion, I believe, was relief that they themselves had not been the subject of Cultt's outburst. You will understand that I felt quite unable to attend his courses again. I left the writing school not in rage and self-confidence as I would wish you to believe, but in despair.

The problem then was where to go. Under no circumstances could I contemplate returning to my parents' home. The literary journalistic world had already taken more notice of the son of an internationally acclaimed novelist embarking on a literary career himself than was comfortable. The failure that they (the journalists, not my parents) had so universally prophesied for me, that was now comprehensively fulfilled, could only reflect adversely upon my father's own career. I took the decision quickly to withdraw the entire contents of my savings account and invest it in supporting myself at some anonymous and affordable location while I considered my alternatives. Thus it was that I travelled to the City and happened upon Mrs. Watkins' rented rooms.

Having installed myself into the temporary security and succour of a heated space within four solid walls, I began doing the only thing I had ever been taught to do. I started to write. The problem now, though, was that having been so undermined I was no longer confident I was capable of writing. I began to look around at the work of other writers – not the literary gods of my youth, but those who were actually succeeding in being published in the modern world. I studied the best of them closely. I listened to short stories on Radio 4 and read the novels that topped the W H Smiths weekly sales lists (particularly those of the summer weeks). I watched children's writers read on CBeebies and spent whole afternoons listening to Poetry Please. Unfortunately nothing suggested itself to me that I could do to make my writing better.

Undeterred, I visited writers' conferences and stood in corners in the foyers where I could observe the best of them gather in learned covens, hoping to overhear them discussing their writers' secrets that only the initiated knew. But upon the prosaic beaches of popular literature the Charles Atlases of genre writing kicked creative sand in my face and I remained a seven stone weakling of the craft. Each evening I would trudge the cobbled streets home and climb the stairs to my rented garret where I would look out over the star-lit city as I thumped away on my old Brother portable typewriter. I worked into the nights, my fingers numb with the growing cold imposed by the coming winter and financial frugality. Yet still I was determined to make myself what I more than half believed I could never be. Failure was as unthinkable as success was inconceivable. In the mornings, Mrs Watkins would find me asleep, slumped over my desk, the floor strewn with screwed up remnants of unfinished scripts, carrion of the previous night's unsuccessful literary hunt.

"You're wrecking your 'ealth, you know, darlin'," she would say to me maternally in that east end accent as she woke me, a pitying look stealing over her old, gnarled face. And I had to admit dear old Mrs Watkins was right. Whatever it was that made real writers what they were, I did not have and could not discover. I was ready to abandon my vocation. I came to a decision: today would be my last day of attempting to be a writer. If, by the end of the day, I had not discovered the elusive secret that gave writers their ability to write, then I would take my typewriter to the second hand shop and give Mrs Watkins what little money I was able to obtain for it in lieu of the many weeks' rent I owed. Then I would write my last will and testament in longhand upon my remaining paper, bequeath my clothing and few personal possessions to some charity for the homeless and cast myself into the river, for my will to live had fled.

Troubled in the extreme and forgetting even to take my pocket watch, I descended the stairs to the street in the hope that the morning sun would somehow cast a shaft of illumination onto my miserable desolation. As I opened the door the sun streamed onto the mosaic floor of the hallway and I stepped outside, blinking in the sudden brightness. Was it my confusion, my state of mind or perhaps the very heart of desperation that beat so insistently in my breast that made me see the alleyway opposite the house that I had never noticed before? I cannot say. But for want of any other purpose to my day, I determined to explore the little turning. With high, windowless walls that largely prevented the penetration of sunlight, it twisted almost immediately to the left, such that I could not see where it led without entering it. My natural inquisitiveness took me forward a few paces until, finding myself in the shadows once more, I blinked to adjust my eyes to the reduced light level. It was only thus in my altered state that I glanced back towards the sunlight and, looking upwards, noticed the name plate of this little road was Meta Lane.

My curiosity thus further excited, I moved on into the darkened alley. Presently, it widened a little, broadening into a street lined with small shops on either side, each of which proffered the passing citizen a variety of plentiful produce of every possible kind. However, at no point could I see more than a few yards ahead of me, for the street continued to twist and turn, this way and that, quite confusing me as to my direction of travel. Here and there large puddles littered the cobbles, remnants of some earlier shower of rain that I had evidently missed. Looking down into their shimmering waters, I watched my distorted reflection jump them – an unusual perspective I had never considered before. A few moments later the lane took a sharp and final turn to the right, whereupon I was met with a dead end. Confronting me was an establishment, a vendor whose precise nature I could not readily determine, for its windows boasted no items immediately familiar to my eye. The name of the establishment written above the entrance read, somewhat incongruously, 'Meta bought, sold and exchanged. The admission of blindness is the beginning of sight.' Assuming myself to be at the premises of some philosophically disposed person and thus intrigued, I reached for the door handle and entered, the little bell on the doorpost sounding a familiar ring.

Inside, the shop was fitted as would befit any retail premises of the modern age. A long counter with a glass top stretched the full width of the room, the wall behind which was lined with drawers that one might reasonably have assumed contained small items – perhaps collar studs, computer memory sticks and other similar appendages. Behind the counter stood a young man, pince-nez upon his nose and his hair receding in advance of his years so as to belie his true youth. It was only later that I came to remark upon the similarity of his appearance and apparent disposition to my own. On his lapel he wore a large, circular badge that declared him to be my 'Personal Assistant', and 'Happy to Help'. When *my assistant* opened his mouth to speak, I was expecting to hear the familiar 'May I be of assistance, sir?' Instead, I was very much taken aback when he leaned over the counter to look me directly in the eye and, smoothing his bald pate, said in a surprisingly familiar tone, "When it's been crafted by an expert, you can't see the join, you know." He stopped momentarily and looked at me enquiringly, as if expecting a response. On receiving none beyond my confused countenance he continued, still eyeing me as directly as if he were my social equal. "We've come for our Meta at last then, have we, Sir?" Indeed, so surprised was I at that moment, that although I opened my mouth to speak, I discovered myself lacking the necessary words to respond. Nor was *my assistant* slow to capitalise upon my confusion, for he seized the moment by continuing, "Come along, Sir, we don't have all day, do we? There's work to be done, Sir, work! Now let's see, I'm certain we have one here to fit us."

And with that he turned his back quite rudely upon me and strode purposefully to the far end of the glass counter. That the latter reflected my image faithfully and intensely, yet his not at all I put down to some trick of the light in the poor illumination of both the establishment and the alley. Reaching the end of the counter, *my assistant* mounted a set of moveable steps in order to reach to the upper level of draws and, stretching my hand over the edge of the highest one, brought forth the item he had evidently been seeking. He descended the steps and strode confidently back to the centre of the shop where, with not a little flourish of triumph, I placed the item down on the glass counter in front of me. I then took a pace back and smiled at me with evident self-satisfaction. "'There we are, Sir," *my assistant* said, "our very own Meta, release 4.0 and much improved, if I may say, on the previous 3.2 model. May it bring us deep and lasting joy," and looked at me expectantly.

With continuing surprise I peered down upon the little item that even now I am not confident I am able to describe accurately, save to say that it appeared to be prismatic, so as to refract such sunlight as was able to make its way into the shop. It cast a shimmering spectrum of light upon the glass topped counter in front of me, tinting my reflection in a most unusual range of shades and causing me to see myself as I had never done before. It was not at all of the nature of an item I might reasonably have expected to discover in a gentleman's outfitters. Suppressing my confusion, finally I was able to compose myself. I opened my mouth to speak. "Precisely," I asked, "what is a Meta for?"

"'Exactly my point, Sir," I replied without hesitation. To this I could think of no suitable reply. Though I considered the possibility of simply exiting the establishment at that moment and walking away, I remained uncomfortably convinced that I should depart in possession of this little item rather than without it. I therefore recovered it from the counter and reached for my wallet in order to make payment. "Oh, there's no charge for it," I said. "'It's ours already. Always has been, so to speak, Sir. Off we go now, and good luck with the writing." I needed no further instruction. Placing the Meta 4.0 into my pocket I left the shop and walked back the length of the alley to the familiar sunlit streets of the city, my heart strangely gladdened.

Having forgotten to put my watch on I couldn't be sure of the time, but judging by the position of the sun it was close to midday. I walked back in the direction of Mrs Watkins' and my room. Unlocking my door I proceeded immediately to my laptop and, ignoring the morning's emails, I took out the Meta 4.0 and placed it on the desk by the computer. Regrettably, it appears to have come without an instruction manual and with no obvious USB connection. However, I am quite certain that when I have discovered how to connect the Meta 4.0 to my work, it will enable me to produce page after page of sublime prose and gain recognition as a real writer. And I shall at last be worthy of my parents' faith in me.

12 Only Three Billion Dreams

There were once identical twin brothers named Alfonse and Bartholomew. No two brothers were closer.

It was unthinkable to both twins that they should ever be separated, so they chose to attend the same provincial university in the north of the country. The visionary Alfonse decided to study politics and sociology. Bartholomew, ever the pragmatist, settled on engineering and economics.

Sadly, on the day that the twins were to be formally awarded their degrees, their parents suffered a fatal road accident. As the boys eventually emerged from their grief it came to light that their parents had left their sons a substantial sum of money. Together the twins gave much thought to what would be done with it. Bartholomew favoured the establishment of an educational foundation in their parents' names. However, Alfonse conceived a truly grand idea. The money would be spent on buying an island in the Caribbean to found a perfect society. "It will be called 'Alfonse's Island'," he told his brother excitedly as he explained his plan to Bartholomew, "and the society we create will be called 'Utopia'." Bartholomew tried not to feel hurt that Alfonse was treating the idea as a fait accompli before obtaining his own agreement, nor that he was naming the island after only himself. But for the sake of keeping the peace he said nothing. 'It really doesn't matter to me what he calls it,' he thought. 'What matters is that we work hard enough to make a difference in the world.'

It did not take Alfonse long to find the perfect place. The island he settled on measured approximately two kilometres by one and had fresh water, but had not been lived on for many years. Bartholomew was taken aback at the amount of money Alfonse was proposing to spend, for it would leave them with rather little for transport, tools, fuel and so on. But Alfonse was having none of it. "This is the perfect island on which to build the perfect society," he said. "Nothing but the best will do as a memorial for our dear parents and for us to show the world how to create happiness." Bartholomew simply raised his eyebrows and resolved to work as hard as he needed to in order to create the vision he now shared.

With almost all the remaining money Alfonse acquired a boat which he named *Alfonse on the Water*. "I didn't mean to exclude you, brother," he explained to Bartholomew the next day as he stood by the controls dressed in captain's whites and peaked cap, "but I had to settle on a name at the time of purchase and I said the first thing that came into my head. We'll name the first building we erect after you. I promise." Bartholomew simply raised his eyebrows, dismissed the matter of names as unimportant, and resolved to work harder. The next morning they left the harbour and the life they had known behind. The voyage was fortunately uneventful. Bartholomew offered to teach Alfonse to fish. However Alfonse declined, saying he needed thinking time to plan how they would establish Utopia on *Alfonse's Island*.

One morning as they neared the island, Alfonse rushed out of the saloon clutching a handful of papers. Excitedly he called to his brother to look at his proudest achievement yet – Utopia's first five year plan. Alfonse outlined the main elements of the plan to Bartholomew each evening after Bartholomew had made dinner and cleared up. Bartholomew didn't mind doing the practical work. It gave him time to think about the more mundane matters of how they would establish a reliable power supply, what shelter might be available, what they would eat and so on.

Finally they arrived at *Alfonse's island.* An improbably azure sea lapped at a white sandy beach strewn with coral and conch shells. Bartholomew looked down from the boat into the clear warm water and knew he truly had arrived in paradise. He could not think of anything else he would ever want again but to live in happiness on this amazing island. Alfonse, by contrast, was not quite as impressed. He eyed the broken jetty and a small derelict building at the land end of it suspiciously. Utopia, he thought, might take just a little longer to achieve than he had planned.

The next day they woke with the sun and discussed what to do. Alfonse stood to speak. He lifted his hand in a gesture that Bartholomew thought rather over-dramatised. "The immediate requirement," said Alfonse in a rather formal tone, "is an action plan. It will take me at least the whole of today to complete it."

Bartholomew nodded his understanding. "Is it ok with you if I start unloading some of the supplies?" he asked. "I want to establish a solar power and battery farm up there." He pointed to the highest south facing point of the island. "I think it will take me a couple of days."

"Yes, why not?" agreed Alfonse. "It will keep you from getting bored while I undertake this vital planning work. Just make sure you're back in time to cook supper and clear up."

'I know he's not being patronising,' thought Bartholomew. 'I know he loves me. What do words matter in comparison with love? We're in this together.' And with that he turned to the practical matter of unloading their equipment while Alfonse undertook the more demanding thinking work.

Due to the density of the vegetation, Bartholomew's anticipated 'couple of days' turned into a week, then a second week. But eventually the power supply was reliably established. Bartholomew proudly passed the connection to his brother.

"Oh, thanks," said Alfonse, barely looking up from his plans. "When will the Internet aerial be ready?"

"I'll make it my next job," Bartholomew promised, trying not to be disappointed that Alfonse had not acknowledged his achievement, and resolving to work extra hard to have the Internet connection ready quickly. After all, he knew how important Internet access was to the vital planning work his brother was undertaking.

This created a slight conflict though, because Bartholomew had anticipated that the next priority should have been the planting of food crops, so that when their supplies ran out they would have enough to eat. He decided that the only solution was to split his day. Mornings would be devoted to the Internet mast and afternoons to agriculture. There was no need to tell Alfonse, who was understandably preoccupied with the hugely important work of filling out the detail of his five year strategic plan. As Bartholomew laboured daily at his self-appointed tasks he was grateful that he had Alfonse there to do the difficult planning work of which he had so little knowledge.

It was when the brothers had been on the island for a month that Alfonse announced that he was ready to share with Bartholomew the first step in his five year plan. Bartholomew was required to take the afternoon off so that he could give his full attention to the matter. After Bartholomew had cleared away from lunch, Alfonse ushered him into the darkened saloon of the boat. From the computer, via an expensive looking projector, he projected a PowerPoint presentation entitled:

The Fastest Way to Utopia:
Alfonse's Island
Five Year Plan
Year 1

Alfonse had taken great trouble to make the presentation look professional with boarders, flow charts and downloaded photographs. Bartholomew was truly impressed. "The road to Utopia," Alfonse began, "has to commence with the election of a Government. The reason for this is simple." Bartholomew stared intensely at the presentation and concentrated carefully on his brother's words. "No society," continued Alfonse, "can be Utopian unless it is supported by the democratic vote of the people. Citizens have to be confident that their leaders are enacting plans that the majority have voted for in free and fair elections." Bartholomew nodded enthusiastically, almost certain he nearly understood what his brother meant. "Because our society is so small," continued Alfonse, "we need to fill only one office of state – that of Prime Minister." He looked closely at Bartholomew, who nodded vigorously again, but did not speak. "So to ensure that the election is truly free and fair," continued Alfonse, "we must both stand for office." Bartholomew looked at him a little uncertainly. "And therefore," continued Alfonse, "we must both produce manifestos. Only when this process is complete can the electorate be truly confident in the programme they are voting for." Alfonse sat down. Bartholomew's expression had turned from enthusiasm to uncertainty.

"Will you help me with mine, brother?" he asked. Alfonse did not answer. He just smiled; a smile that some, though not Bartholomew, might have considered patronising.

Alfonse completed his manifesto a week before the election and delivered it to Bartholomew's cabin in an envelope marked with the words 'Electoral Communication'. For his part, Bartholomew had worried for days about what he would write. After all, he had studied engineering which, compared to Alfonse's politics, gave him no preparation for the writing of manifestos. But he knew his brother would be cross if he had nothing to show him, so he jotted a few thoughts down, supported by some mathematical calculations. In tribute to Alfonse's amazing presentation he put a cover sheet on the front of these thoughts and called his manifesto 'The Fastest Way to Utopia: Production in the Utopian Society'. In it he covered some fairly obvious matters. Firstly they would not want to live on the boat for ever; homes would need to be built. Secondly, if they wanted Utopian society to amount to more than just the two of them, they would need to create some form of business venture to attract others to the island to work. Bartholomew suggested a fish processing plant. This could help fund many other necessities such as healthcare or education for any future children.

Alfonse took the document in silence and left the cabin. Ten minutes later he was back, his face red with rage. He snatched his own manifesto out of Bartholomew's hands and stormed out. Late that night the document was pushed back under the door, an addendum having been added addressing the following:
- Production
- Treasury Functions
- Taxation.

But by this time Bartholomew was asleep and did not read the amended manifesto.

The next day the two brothers delivered final election speeches to each other. Alfonse stood in his best suit which Bartholomew had always admired and spoke in oratorical fashion with the aid of PowerPoint slides and an audio track for a full forty-five minutes. When it came to his turn to speak, Bartholomew, dressed in his usual cut-off denims and t-shirt, mumbled just a few words and looked at the floor throughout.

Then the brothers voted in the secret ballot by marking an 'X' on ballot papers that Alfonse had downloaded and printed. As Retuning Officer, Alfonse then declared the poll closed. The next day the votes were counted. Alfonse emptied the ballot box onto the table. Two votes fell out, both folded. Alfonse opened the first. A cross was clearly visible in the box with Alfonse's name next to it. He looked at Bartholomew in silence for a long time. Then, turning away, without opening the second voting slip, he mumbled "Spoiled ballot," screwed up the remaining paper and threw it out of the port hole into the sea. He then declared Alfonse duly elected as Prime Minister of Alfonse's Island, one vote to nil. Bartholomew made no objection. He was asleep. When he awoke later Alfonse was back in his cabin. Bartholomew assumed Alfonse had been elected. He was simply glad the election was over and that he could get back to work.

The next morning Alfonse appeared once again in his suit and tie. Bartholomew was still dressed in the cut-off jeans and t-shirt he had worn the night before. Alfonse, who had clearly been up for hours, handed him a press release announcing the formation of the new state, which he had already issued online, together with a zoning plan, dividing the island into various areas – residential, commercial, civic, agricultural – and an itinerary. The last of these set out a schedule for Alfonse to make a six month trip around the Caribbean to establish diplomatic relations with other states. "I am placing you in charge of Utopia during my absence," he announced to Bartholomew rather grandly. "While I am away you are to concentrate on agriculture and, if you have time, industrialisation."

Bartholomew watched Alfonse back the large motor yacht away from the jetty. He wouldn't really miss the comforts of the boat – the TV, the freezer, the alcohol. In the year they had been on the island he had grown to realise that his happiness did not depend on these things. He had also conceived a plan. He would indeed concentrate on the matters his brother had specified while he was away – agriculture and industrialising their little society with the creation of a fishing and fish packing business. However, in his free time, during the long evenings when he did not have Alfonse to listen to, he would create a permanent home for them both. And this time he was determined to follow Alfonse's lead and plan everything properly. So he started by drawing up a front sheet for his plan that said:

Bartholomew's six months alone
How I will build a fish packing business
And a home

He could not think of much to write after that and rather wished he had Alfonse there to help him. Instead he filled the pages with technical drawings of the fish packing plant and plans for the house he intended to build.

Over the coming days Bartholomew fell into a routine of mornings devoted to tending the crops, afternoons working on the fish packing building and evenings devoted to building a home for himself and his brother. He grew more and more excited about his creations as each week passed. His crops were growing, the fish packing plant was rising before his eyes. But what he was even more proud of was the home he was building. Up on the hillside, it looked down over the jetty with the most fabulous view over the beach towards the setting sun. He had not told Alfonse, but in the agricultural zone he had planted vines and hoped in a few years to be able to produce wine. He dreamed of standing on the veranda of their home with Alfonse, holding a glass of their own Sauvignon, looking out towards the setting Caribbean sun.

Six months of intense labour produced admirable results: food in the store, a business ready to commence and best of all a wonderful home. Finally, as Bartholomew surveyed his labour and looked out to sea, he spotted *Alfonse on the Water* cruising home. He raced down to the jetty. He could see the boat in detail now, his brother at the helm, waving. Then he realised that Alfonse was not alone. Someone was standing next to him; a woman. On arrival, Alfonse jumped down onto the jetty and hugged his brother, then called out to the woman. Chantale came shyly forward and also jumped down, smiled coyly at Bartholomew and shook his hand lightly. "Hello, I am most pleased to meet you," she said in faltering English with a heavy foreign accent.

The three of them walked up to the new house and spent the evening talking by candle light. Alfonse was stunned with the new house. He wandered round the rooms, holding Chantale by the hand, admiring the joinery and craftwork, and in particular the way shafts of evening sunlight filtered through the hallway to fall like sparking rain on the smooth hardwood floors. Later, after Bartholomew had cooked and served a meal, they sat on the veranda, cradling glasses of Sauvignon that Alfonse had brought back and watched the sun sink slowly into the western sea. Bartholomew was bursting with happiness at the fulfilment of his vision.

"It was an incredible trip," began Alfonse. "I was well received everywhere. I was treated so much like a Head of State that I can honestly say I have truly become a Head of State, just like the many I have met around the Caribbean. And Bartholomew, I'm so excited. I have so many incredible new ideas for the development of Utopia. I have a vision," he said, his voice becoming somehow grander, "I have a dream. My dream is one of the development of our society. I see great Ministries of State and a Civil Service to support them. I see a growing reputation in the international community. I see international recognition of our success in building Utopia, awards, accolades; perhaps in time I shall even be awarded a Nobel prize. There will be many reciprocal visits to be paid by the International Community to Utopia. Bartholomew, you need to understand what we're creating here. It's going to be incredible. We're going to be compared with the greatest bureaucracies in the world. Why, even the European Union will visit to learn from us." And he continued to pour out a stream of ideas and plans, leaving Bartholomew breathless and confused as to how all this grandeur could possibly be afforded. Finally Alfonse came to the most difficult issue. "But brother, there's something I've got to explain to you. I don't want you to think that I don't appreciate all this amazing work you've done while I've been away. I'm delighted you've been able to keep boredom at bay in my absence and I love this wonderful house in particular. But there's just one problem, dear brother. You've built the house in the Civic Zone that has been set aside for Government buildings. I'm grateful, truly grateful for the preparatory work you've started. And it's just as well the building has not been properly fitted out yet, because unfortunately this house can't be used for domestic habitation by non-government employees." Bartholomew listened in respectful silence as his brother explained the concepts of zoning and the importance of keeping to rules once they had been set. He nodded when Alfonse reminded him that he had been democratically elected by the people to look after the interests of all citizens of Utopia in the way he considered would be best for all, not just those who had voted for him. He hid his disappointment very well indeed.

Finally, Alfonse concluded, "The house will, however, make a fine seat of Government. I want to honour your work, brother, by making it the Prime Minister's official residence and calling it the White House. I promise it will carry a plaque declaring your involvement in the early phases of its construction. And don't worry, there's no urgency to paint it white. You can leave it until next week if you're too busy until then."

The next morning Bartholomew left before first light, leaving Alfonse and Chantale to sleep in after their long voyage. He stowed the fishing gear on *Alfonse on the Water* and turned the boat out of the little natural harbour and motored out to a promising fishing ground on the east side of the island. Soon he had the boat's rear locker full of fish. He returned to the jetty just as the sun was rising, unloading straight into the processing plant. He then considered a problem that he knew he would face – who would process the fish? He could not simultaneously tend the crops, go fishing and process the catch. So he decided to ask Alfonse if Chantale would be willing to help. Coincidentally, at that moment Alfonse and Chantale arrived at the jetty, arm in arm, laughing. Bartholomew immediately put the idea to Alfonse. Alfonse drew a deep breath and turned bright red, his eyed bulging. At first Bartholomew thought he was having a seizure. Then he roared in fury, "Brother! Do you realise what you're asking? You can't possibly, possibly be serious. Don't you understand the risks you're asking me to take with such a suggestion? Chantale's work permit for Utopia covers only government sponsored work. And besides, her English isn't good enough. As a prospective employer you simply couldn't consider placing her in a position of responsibility. And Bartholomew, what can you possibly be thinking of? The worst of your suggestion is that dear Chantale has received no health and safety training, What if she were to injure herself and sue? Utopia could be wiped out by such carelessness before it's been properly established." Alfonse finally finished his tirade. He looked angrily at his brother for what Bartholomew thought was the first time in their lives. For his part, Bartholomew was contrite. He had had no idea of the potential consequences of the course of action he had intended to take. He dropped the idea immediately.

That day he processed as many fish as he could, but much of the catch had to be dumped back into the ocean. As he prepared supper for Alfonse and Chantale in the White House kitchen that evening he wondered what to do. And then an idea came to him. Later, back in the fish plant he allowed himself the sparing use of some electricity for lighting and prepared a written plan to submit to Alfonse in the morning. It was entitled

Employment in Utopia
A Proposal to the Prime Minister

Bartholomew filled the following pages with arguments for recruiting a small work force that would be permitted to live on the island and work in the fish plant. He even covered the commercial implications of needing to find buyers and transport for the fish. Both recruitment and sales would be conducted via the Internet. The next morning after tending the agricultural zone at first light, he returned to the boat, put on his best clothes and strode to the door of the White House at precisely 9.00 am clutching his proposal. On the door was a new sign that read:

The White House, Utopia
Citizens may consult the Government between the hours of 10.00 am and 3.00 pm on Tuesdays and Thursdays.

Fortunately, it was a Tuesday. When Chantale answered the door, Bartholomew asked if he could see Alfonse. She indicated a chair in the hall that he himself had made and walked away. An hour later she returned, and showed him into the room he had intended to be the dining room. Here Alfonse sat, suited, behind the dining table that Bartholomew had painstakingly carved. He stood up immediately. "Bartholomew!" he exclaimed. "How marvellous to see you, old bean! Do sit down. What can I do for you?" Bartholomew passed his document across the table. Alfonse sat back in his chair and glanced through it quickly. "Very interesting, old chap," he said as he laid the final page face down. "Many complications you've not thought of, of course. But that's to be expected. Let my people take a look at it and we'll get back to you."

Little happened for the next month... in fact for the next two months. Bartholomew tended the agricultural zone and caught as many fish as he knew he could process, but in truth they had more than enough in the freezer to last the three of them a long time. At the end of each day he would climb up to the White House, trying not to feel envious, and cook supper for the three of them, then return to *Alfonse on the Water* to sleep. One morning when he returned from fishing, there was a manila envelope propped up against the door to the saloon with the words printed in bold red letters,

State of Utopia
Official Government Papers
Eyes Only

Bartholomew wasn't sure what 'eyes only' meant and wondered if there was some other way of reading words other than with your eyes. Nevertheless, he opened the envelope and took out a pack of papers entitled:

Utopia Development Plan
Year 2
Production, Employment, Monetary System and Taxation

That evening he settled down to read the garrulous document. On the third reading he finally managed to catch on to its main thread – Utopia should now concentrate on expansion by bringing in workers from overseas to fulfil the ever growing work load of the ministries of state. In order to ensure workers' rights were established upon Utopian principles from the beginning, the following would be enshrined in law:

- A Bill of Rights would be passed by Parliament.

- Employment of workers other than under the state specified system would be a criminal offence punishable by fine and/or imprisonment.
- All workers would be given the right to establish a small homestead on a specified plot in the residential zone. Planning laws would specify the size and type of building permitted.
- Workers would be divided into state employees and private sector employees.
- There would be a minimum wage (though state employees would receive a higher 'living wage').
- In addition to the legal minimum holiday entitlement of twenty-five days per year for all workers, state workers would also be entitled to additional state holidays to which private sector employees were not entitled.
- Private sector employers would be obliged to pay into a state sponsored pension scheme for their workers, monitored by a Regulator. State employees would be entitled to more advantageous pension rights than the employees of private sector employers.
- Prospective employers would be permitted to apply for an employment license for each employee, their engagement being subject to thorough suitability and entitlement to work checks.
- Employees would be entitled to workers' rights from date of employment, including:
  - Protection from unfair dismissal,
  - Parenting and dependant relative rights,
  - Health and safety rights,
  - Training rights,
  - Pension rights.
- Another Regulator would be appointed to monitor private sector employer compliance with these requirements with fines and/or imprisonment for non-compliant employers.
- All employers would be required to draw up general health and safety policies and procedures to protect the welfare of their workers. This would include, amongst other things, such matters as
  - Safety in industrial processes

- Dangers of VDUs (though Bartholomew could think of only three on the island)
- Design of work stations
- Design of chairs
- Maximum work periods, working hours and minimum rest days
- Freedom from stress
- Specific rights relating to vision for night workers
- Health assessments if requested by employees.

The list continued interminably with references to risk assessments, action plans, fire policies, sickness pay, parental leave, anti-discrimination laws, premises licensing and many other matters, until Bartholomew finally fell asleep over it.

When he awoke he was saddened by the state's presumption that employers would exploit their workers unless compelled otherwise by law, for he was by nature a generous person and concerned for the welfare of others. But he was even more daunted by the sheer volume of work he would need to undertake if he wished to employ people. He still believed unswervingly that the best contribution he could make to the establishment of Utopia would be a commercial one. Yet in this proposed system of organisation, commerce would be strangled at birth by the amount of 'compliance activity' required, preventing him and his future employees from being productive. However, the white paper had even dealt with this issue, for it proposed that all employers take on, as their very first employee, a Compliance Officer (who would, naturally, qualify for all employment rights themselves upon engagement) in order to create the records that would evidence the business's compliance with the requirements of the state.

By the time Bartholomew had finished reading, it was obvious to him that Utopia regarded producers as dangerous people that needed to be controlled carefully; people who must be given only obligations and no rights. But he saw no point in arguing with the democratically elected government. These proposals were now as good as law. He had no alternative but to comply – and then if he failed, even for innocent reasons, he might well still be fined or imprisoned.

At precisely 10.00 am that Thursday he called at the White House to ask for application papers to employ immigrant workers. Filling in and returning the papers took a further week. A week after that Bartholomew received another manila envelope, this time containing copies of his application papers stamped and dated with a rather officious looking seal of state.

Many weeks and another harvest later, the 'Certificate of Approval of Employer Status' arrived in yet another manila envelope. Fortunately Bartholomew had been able to get ahead while waiting, by using the old laptop computer from the boat to begin advertising on the Internet for both staff and customers. He had filled the packing plant's freezer room with a consignment that was ready for sale and had found a customer for it. The whole contents of the freezer were due to be collected that Wednesday.

The collecting vessel that arrived was three times the size of *Alfonse on the Water.* It manoeuvred, with some difficulty, alongside the jetty. Bartholomew realised that he needed to improve the facilities as soon as it was affordable if he was to make a success of the new commercial venture. That would no doubt require all the funds he was generating from this sale and several more to follow. The fish were loaded and Bartholomew handed over the invoice to the Captain – $5,000 for immediate cash settlement. The captain smiled and passed him a wad of notes. They shook hands and the vessel headed out to sea. Unbeknown to Bartholomew, standing on the veranda of the White House was Alfonse, observing the proceedings through a pair of expensive binoculars.

Twenty-four hours later a further manila envelope appeared at the door. This time it contained only two sheets of paper. On the first was printed a short paragraph:

The State of Utopia confirms the establishment of the following:

- Government Treasury, responsible for collection of taxes and payment of Government liabilities, situated at The White House.
- The new unit of currency, which will be called the Utopian *Dream* with an official exchange rate of 1 Dream to the US $.

- The immediate imposition of the following rates of tax;
    - Sales Tax   20%
    - Corporation tax   20%
    - Income tax   25%
    - Employer's National Insurance   5%
    - Employee's National Insurance   5%

The second piece of paper was a tax demand requiring him to declare all relevant income for the period ending that day and to pay the required tax.

Bartholomew sighed heavily and climbed slowly up to the White House where the door was opened even before he arrived by the Prime Minster himself. "Brother! How good it is to see you," he said. "I do hope you've been keeping well. I'm so sorry it has not been possible for us to meet recently but you know how it is, affairs of state and so on."

Bartholomew was pleased to see his brother of course, but not so thrilled to have to pay the unexpected tax. However, Alfonse, on behalf of the state, generously waived his liability to National Insurance and took from him only $1,000 in sales tax, $800 in Corporation Tax and $800 in Income Tax. This left Bartholomew with $2,400 for his work, his expenditure and to meet the investment needs of his business. Alfonse congratulated him on receiving his permits to commence business and asked him how trade was. Indeed, Alfonse didn't even charge him for the iced tea they drank while seated on the veranda, so Bartholomew had to agree with his brother in the end, that the state had treated him very fairly indeed.

At this point Bartholomew stopped work entirely and devoted all his time to completion of the vast array of paperwork that the state now required before he could employ people. He set up recruitment systems, undertook risk assessments, applied for operation permits, wrote employment manuals and health and safety manuals and did everything else required to be able to engage workers. Finally he submitted his applications to the White House together with a rather hefty fee and waited. And while he waited and waited, a second collection of fish was made by his customer. Another $5,000 was paid to him, another manila envelope with another tax demand arrived, another payment of $2,600 in tax was made.

At precisely 10.00 am one morning there was a knock on the door of the fish processing unit. Bartholomew answered to find a complete stranger standing there – a tall, balding man of about fifty years of age with a moustache. Round his neck he had an identity tag which, without uttering a word, he held up to Bartholomew. It read, 'State of Utopia Authorised Regulator'. Suitably impressed, Bartholomew stepped aside to permit entry to the Regulator who had come to conduct an inspection . He refused several offers of refreshment, toured the premises once and then sat down to examine Bartholomew's paperwork. At precisely 4.30 pm the visitor announced he had not finished his inspection but would return 'another day in the near future' to continue.

The next morning at 10.00 am precisely, there was another knock on the door. A young woman in a business suit held up an identification card to him. This also said 'Regulator.' The woman explained that her colleague who called the previous day was abroad attending an international cluster group on the future of intercontinental collaboration in regulation and she had come to complete the inspection. Bartholomew had never heard of a cluster group, much less an international one, but it sounded impressive. By 1.00 pm the Regulator pronounced herself satisfied with the inspection and left. Bartholomew settled down to catch up on the work he had missed due to the visits.

Finally authorised to proceed with employing a work force and expanding the business, Bartholomew decided to celebrate by permitting himself a walk round the island. As he rounded a headland he was confronted by an extraordinary sight. Upwards of a dozen small buildings were in the process of construction, each exactly the same, each being worked on by one or two people. Several uniformed individuals stood watching and comparing notes they were all keeping on clipboards. Bartholomew looked down towards the sea where he was surprised to see another jetty had been built and several boats were tied up.

To Bartholomew this was one step too far. He strode defiantly to the White House where Alfonse was seated on the veranda drinking iced tea. Bartholomew demanded an explanation for all these new people on their island.

Alfonse was entirely un-phased by his brother's anger. He simply replied, "My dear Bartholomew, there's no secret here. What you see is your tax Dreams at work for you! These are authorised foreign workers employed by the government of Utopia under recognised work permits. But I'm glad you've come to see me, old fellow, because there's a small problem I need to discuss with you. We've rather stretched the budget getting all these people here and the Treasury's fallen a bit short of funds. So we've decided to issue some ten year 5% government bonds to fund all the coming expenditure on developing the state. And, er, by the way I'm afraid that all the land designated for residential development for the next five years is now allocated to state employees, so there would be nowhere to house private sector workers if you were planning to engage any. And, oh, unfortunately, if you don't commence an employment business within twelve months of the granting of your permits they expire and you'll have to apply again."

Bartholomew looked his brother in the eyes for a long, long time. Then he asked, "How much are you borrowing?"

"Oh, only three billion Dreams," replied Alfonse, "which is less than 75% of projected GDP for year four of the five year plan." Bartholomew continued looking at Alfonse for a long time without speaking. Finally, without uttering another word, he turned and walked down the hill.

That evening he loaded onto the boat as much agricultural produce and frozen fish as he could manage, locked the processing plant and threw the key into the harbour. Then he got on the boat and turned it towards the open sea.

As the *Alfonse on the Water* pulled away from the shore a powerful motorboat with a flashing blue light approached him at considerable speed. Bartholomew stopped his engines. The vessel came along side and the *Alfonse* was immediately boarded by a man in a peaked cap and a blue uniform. "Sorry to trouble you, sir," he said. "Could I please see your departure permit?"

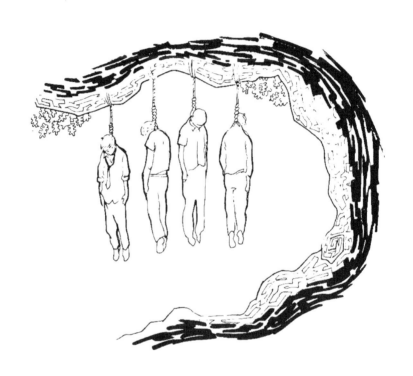

13 Served Cold

I first noticed Will as he sat quietly at the back of the class, ignoring the taunts of the biggest bullies of our year. They hated him for the pleasure of hating and taunted him for the clean white shirts his mam insisted he wore every Monday and Thursday. They abused him most of all because he would not risk those ill-afforded shirts to cross the brook on the rope we'd strung from the old oak that leaned out over the water. Tommy and Mikey and Freddie and Pete leaped from the high earth bank, the rope spinning beneath them like some rabid viper as they struggled and jerked their way towards the other side. Will simply looked on silently, as they derided him without mercy, drawing his pain back into a furnace that lingered raw and red upon his cheeks. Only now do I realise what he was thinking as he watched them screaming and giggling on that rope.

There was a kind of nobility about him then that towered up above his years, too high and lofty for his tormentors to see. I loved him for his respect for his mam and for those Thursday shirts and the heart that he always wore just inside his sleeve. Never once did he soil his soul by responding to the ignominy they poured on him in bucket loads from the reassuring altitude of pack scorn.

In the way that young boys always did and always shall do, they tormented Will relentlessly up through the lock gates of each succeeding school year until they reached the high mountain lakes of fourteen. Then they all launched themselves out on an unsuspecting world of would-be adulthood, seeking greater sport than could be gotten from abusing the different and the better and the noble and the good. But by that time it was too late for Will. A man may choose silence over confrontation, tears over fists for year after year, but there always remains a wave mark in the sand, invisible to all but himself. Force him across that line and the tides of self-preservation will wash away his goodness forever. And if you inflict that kind of metamorphosis upon him, be prepared to joust with the devil for the rest of his days.

As puberty prepared Will for adulthood, the butterfly that finally spluttered and struggled out of his chrysalis was malformed and grotesque. A black beacon of hatred shone from behind his eyes like some satanic neon in the space where the light and the love and the joy were supposed to be. Without warning he changed his name from Will to Bill and his disposition from gentle patience to incandescent rage. It was then that he gave himself to bruising his knuckles on weaker chins and honing his malevolence on the souls of the easily manipulated.

His mam never saw the blood on his hands or the darkness in his heart when he returned home from the dance halls on a Saturday night. For like the werewolf he must really have been, by Sunday morning he had changed. He would be down in the best room waiting for her when the grandmother chimed a quarter to ten, another clean white shirt on his shoulders and an impenetrable shroud over his soul. In his hand he would clutch a Bible that spoke of the God he loathed, while he parodied the dutiful son, accompanying his mother to Matins. And if, somewhere deep in the dungeon of that dark ego, an emaciated goodness was rattling on the bars to get out, well, I never saw it.

Perhaps it was fitting that they came for him on a Sunday. He showed neither resistance nor repentance when they shackled him and took him down to the brook where the high oak still stood, its branches reaching silently out over the water. Four ropes hung there, taught and still under the weights they bore. Nothing but the gurgling brook broke the silence of the morning.

I can only surmise that on the preceding evening those ropes, too, had spun like vipers, as Tommy and Mikey and Freddie and Pete struggled and jerked their way to the other side of eternity and whatever reward or punishment awaited them.

No one but Will's mam was surprised at what he had done. And she never could understand when he said that it was for her that he had done it. So great was her terror when she stared into the salivating fangs of the truth, that she did not live long enough to see him locked away, back in the days when life really did mean life.

So I guess it must be true. The universe really is ruled by a just and merciful God after all.

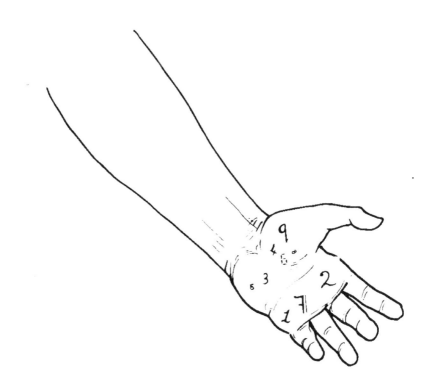

14   The Immortal

When I was young I was immortal. My father was the sun and my mother the moon. Together they shone upon me by day and by night so that never should I see darkness descend.

But while I slept the sun came to me in a dream. Upon his hands he carried numbers that cast the weight of six blue digits, fading secrets of the canticles of time. And though the sun and the moon knew the purpose of the numbers, they had long conspired that this secret would not be shared. No, not even in whispers would they share, lest the heart of my sister Venus be troubled or my brother Mars the warmonger overhear and become enraged.

I hung my immortality upon a hook, and fled the skies to seek the purpose of the numbers. At the university I sought out skilled mathematicians, but though they understood much, the reason for the creation of the digits confounded them. I turned to the greatest physicists, but they, too, were without explanation. And while I pondered the teaching of ancient philosophies, none offered an explanation for the creation of the shimmering, fading numbers.

In my frustration I turned away from learning and in time amassed much wealth. But each night the numbers shimmered before my eyes and I was without peace until once more I gave myself to their quest.

Years passed. My body wearied. Learning grew. But no wisdom came to offer purpose to the numbers.

Now all my learning is outdated. The wealth has dissipated and in my flesh I know weariness beyond my ability to tell.

When I was young I was immortal.

My father came to me in a dream, six faded blue digits tattooed upon his forearm.

It was my father who taught me how to die.

15   The Man Who Spoke to the Dryads

My paternal grandfather was an English shaman with a profound connection to the dryads. My mother, at the age of seventeen, fell in love with him as soon as they met. This was at the first Beltane festival ever to be held just outside Malvern in 1961 where she offered herself to him immediately.

There were some understandable reasons for this. Not only was she, at the time, of an age when she was wide open to the possibility of falling in love, but it was also acknowledged by almost all who knew him that my grandfather was a man who radiated sexual attraction. In his youth he stood well in excess of six feet six tall. It was only after a lifetime of stooping over the harvest, rodent traps and his clients, that necessity bestowed upon him an intermittent requirement to walk bent at a forty-five degree angle. However, until those later years this rural giant stood erect and proud, as many surviving monochrome photographs still attest. The same photos confirm my personal recollection that he had one of the most unusual faces I have ever seen. With a long, angular nose, a narrow mouth and the most powerful of horn rimmed spectacles, this was clearly not a face such as one might expect women to fall in love with. But it was one that wore an expression of intensity, wisdom and power. It was these characteristics, I believe, that were later to account for deep disturbances in the energy fields of both of them, of the family and of the karmic line.

Being that we were a family steeped in generations of traditional witchcraft, we were amongst the first to make a public commitment to the new religion that flourished in thean unusually territorial individual for one so skilled in the ways of the Craft, made it clear that my mother's selfless offer, though admirable, was not going to be accepted by her husband. Instead, she introduced the young woman immediately to her own son. Clearly taking after his father, he was a tall, angular youth of nineteen who put all who saw him in mind of an under-watered oak sapling.

The surviving photographs of my mother from this era attest to the commonly acknowledged observation that teenage girls are often more sexually developed than teenage boys of a similar age. With flowing black hair that reached the middle of her back, dark eyes, and a petite but hour-glass figure she might, in a different life, have become a model. As it was, for this lifetime her contract was what we might now refer to as Wiccan and by her fifteenth birthday she was wont to dance naked before Adonis under the grey light of the harvest moon.

My mother was less than delighted at the proffered substitution of my father for her first choice, but recognised the potential it offered for subsequent interaction with the real target of her hormonal disruption. The betrothal was formalised at Glastonbury during the Mabon dance offering, where she was renamed Persephone and he Bacchus. It was not surprising that Persephone's new name became that by which she was known for the rest of her life. By contrast, once Bacchus had heard a number of people giggles when introduced to him, he reverted to his original given name of Alan, shortened to Al. By Yule his Coven name had lapsed entirely.

Grandfather himself was named as William Peter Dente in his year of birth of 1926 and did not take a Craft name. A man of Mediterranean ancestry, and one for whom the world was a very serious place, he never did see the potential for humour in his choice of name for his son. Grandmother was named for the abundant provision of the Earth Spirits long before any thought was given to her eventual name change upon marriage. Her own parents cannot therefore be held responsible for the subsequent mildly humorous consequences upon marriage of having given her the name of Plenty.

William and Plenty were Somerset farmers who hailed from the rural community to the west of Frome and whose outlook on life they largely shared. Most people who tendered currency at the market instead of bartering were considered to be potentially attempting to cheat them. Virtually anyone originating from across the county boundary two miles to the east of Frome was in essence foreign. And absolutely anyone who pronounced Frome to rhyme with home rather than room was considerably less intelligent than any member of their rapidly fattening herd of pigs.

I do not mean to imply by this that my grandparents were ignorant – quite the reverse. Each of them possessed an unquestionable empathy with the natural world. William was known throughout the county as a Cunning Man of great power such as in more recent years would be called a shaman, and in particular for his ability to heal with earth energy. To watch him at work was nothing short of a joy. He would have his clients lie supine on the floor, place them into trance with a combination of murmured incantations and slow fixated breathing that few could resist the inclination to imitate. Once he had achieved what he considered to be an effective connection to the patient's higher self, he would assist them in drawing energy down from the light. I and my contemporaries who heal in much the same way talk of crown chakra, solar plexus and the like. But William knew nothing of these terms. He had this way – and I have never been able to replicate it – of circulating the energy and accelerating it and, as it were, throwing it to whichever part of the physical or astral body was expressing distress. This he referred to as *'spinnin' th' cauldron.'*

In the all the years I watched him work I never once saw his technique fail. By the time he had finished, his client would invariably be asleep. Then, upon rousing, a short period of disorientation would follow. William would sit them in the farmhouse garden. Here they would re-orientate on a seat he had carved from the stump of an old elm tree that had died in the attack of Dutch elm disease in the late 1960s. Or if it were winter they would sit in front of the ever-burning fire in the kitchen inglenook and drink unceasing glassfuls of Plenty's elderflower cordial. Payment would occasionally be in the form of money. But in truth William and Plenty had little use for currency. It was much preferred if the grateful client would leave behind them a chicken or two, or perhaps return later to mend a fence or a cartwheel, depending on the wealth, skill or calling of the individual concerned.

Let me state clearly the significance to my grandparents of that attack of Dutch elm disease that commenced in 1967. Of the two of them it was William who was more deeply affected, for he was the one with the ability to communicate directly with the dryads. Nevertheless, Plenty was very much of the same mind and had a more systemic connection to the children of the earth – her animals, her birds and even the insects for which she exhibited an enduring respect. I never once saw her kill anything other than out of pure necessity or to end suffering. There was to be much suffering and homelessness exhibited throughout the animal kingdom with the arrival of the Elmish infection. So strong was William's connection that the trees themselves had made him aware of the impending incursion of the dreaded disease upon our shores from 1965, some two years before its actual arrival.

I might also mention almost as a footnote to this much more important narrative, the marriage of my parents in 1962 and the birth of me, their first child, in 1963. At eighteen Persephone was perhaps not so unusually young a mother. But at twenty, Al was surely too young to be a father. I have always sought to forgive Al's abandonment of her and me a little before my fifth birthday, considering it as being attributable to too early an entry into parenthood. Unsurprisingly Persephone was, for many years, unable to share what she regarded as far too charitable an interpretation of Al's departure as I chose to make. Additionally, I was demonstrably too young at the time to interpret the significance of his preoccupation with a traveller girl who passed through Frome that summer, en route to the Solstice celebration in Glastonbury. But whatever the interpretation, the fact was that one morning in mid-June the traveller caravans were gone and so was he.

Given that we all lived together on the farm anyway, and in particular in view of the amount of time I was wont to spend with William, Al's departure had far less impact upon me than might otherwise have been the case. Regrettably, the same was not true for Persephone, who at the age of twenty-three was barely an adult herself. It was predictable that her husband's desertion would initially cause grief and anguish. Perhaps with the benefit of hindsight it should have been equally predictable that the emotional confusion of his leaving would lead to further disruption within the extended family.

Al's departure coincided with the approach of my fifth birthday, which engendered much discussion within the family as regards the nature and style of education I was to receive.

William was forthright upon the matter. "We don' see no call fer booklarnin', " he ventured. "My granfer' an' my dard din' get none and neither did we. An' we'm not seein' why 'e need be wasstin' 'is time in the schoolarse."

Nevertheless, we were living in an era in which the authorities took rather more interest in the delivery of *booklarnin* that had been the case during William's childhood.

"Oh, don't be givin' me that, Dad," Persephone replied. "The world's been changin' since your day. I think school learnin' will be good for the boy. And anyways, he be my son an' I'll be decidin' what be good for 'im."

Given that Plenty was broadly of the same opinion as her daughter-in-law, it was determined that I would, just prior to Mabon, attend at the *Schoolarse* in Frome along with the other children of the local community.

As I have already mentioned, William had prior warning of the arrival of Dutch elm disease upon the English shores in 1967. It had constituted, as he put it, 'T'only inn'rcourse 'tween Elm and Dryad' since that date, and one entered into with progressively more fear as time had passed. The English dryads were in systemic contact with their fellows in North America where the disease had already taken hold. In 1967 the actual arrival of the elm bark beetle in a shipment of Rock Elm logs from North America led to a tsunami of arboreal panic that swept across the country from south to north. This emotional wave was to be followed by the death of twenty-five million Elm trees out of a national population of thirty million.

Thus, for two years William did what he could to prepare his beloved trees for the coming storm, which, in honesty, was little. And with its arrival in 1967 he and other dryad-connected humans did what they could to move the energy in favour of the trees and away from the beetles. But the inexorable march of the invertebrates was beyond even his powerful majik. Empathetic humans and dryads of other tree species looked on helplessly as their fellows wept inconsolably, wandering aimlessly amongst their dead flocks.

It was in this context that William arrived at the decision in the summer of 1968 that he would begin my training as what we would call in our generation a dryadic shaman. Neither of us could have realised at that time just how important that learning was to be. For, as it later transpired, my training was to prepare me for intervention into a terrifying conflict between humanity and the dryads which at that time none of us could have foreseen.

On the night of the full moon of July 1968 he woke me from my bed, dressed me and led me deeper into the forest than I had ever been before. As we journeyed onwards I became aware that I was treading territory that I had never previously crossed. Suddenly William let go my hand and strode on into the darkness at an adult's pace I was incapable of matching. My reaction to this was surprise rather than fear. Already the forest was a home to me, a haven of nurturing rather than a threat. But it had rained heavily that day. The ground was soft and the terrain uneven and sloping. Though my eyes had adjusted to the moonlight and I could see, the problem was simply that I didn't know where I was. Then, as I slipped and slithered my way forward, I was suddenly aware that I was not alone. Just as I was losing my balance I felt a presence on each side of me. I turned to the right to confront the first, but could see nothing. As I turned back towards my left confusingly, the presence on my right came into view while that on my left remained oddly invisible. What I was experiencing was the concentration of rod cells in the edges of the human eye and cones at its centre. It was my first lesson in seeing peripherally that which cannot be seen face on – a lesson that all should learn at least metaphorically, even if not physically. As I adjusted to this new means of visual perception I was better able to see the physical presences that were assisting me. Each was a creature larger than me, but well short of the full height of an adult human. Thin and angular, with bony faces, horizontal, slit-like eyes and sharp chins, they put me first in mind of skeletons. Yet these creatures were very much alive, and as they gently touched and supported me it was clear that they were well-intentioned towards me. With them as much carrying me forward as leading me, we advanced into a clearing that I had never realised existed. There in the centre stood my grandfather, naked. And around him, now that I had the eyes to see in the grey moonlight, perhaps two dozen other creatures similar in appearance to those who had taken charge of me.

My training began that full-mooned night with a history lesson. As William sought to expound to me the *"hist'ry o' th' dryads"* many interruptions took place as dryad after dryad extended bony hands and fingers to touch my soft skin, or to stroke my hair, or inhale my scent, much as we might run our fingers over pine needles or inhale the perfume of the swaying trees on a warm summer afternoon.

"You needs t'unnerstand," he said in his broad Somerset voice, "that Dryads work with trees as shepherds do with sheep. Each man'ges a flack o' between a dozen and a hunert trees. But it's a two-way matter, you sees. The trees'll not prosper without the nurturing of t' dryads. But t'dryads also can't live without t'trees."

Indeed, while few humans really have a genuine appreciation of this, the dryad symbiosis with the trees is not that different from our own.

"Two thousand years ago," he continued, "this were covered by forest, mostly oak. But with the comin' of t'Romans and the creep o' 'uman civilisation, the great forests was driven back."

To the dryads this has always been a matter of considerable confusion, experiencing as they do, the immediacy of our shared dependency upon the trees. Why, they perpetually ask me, do we destroy the very source of oxygen upon which our own survival depends?

I had no answer for them back then and I have none now. And who can blame the dryads if they regard the tiny forested areas such as the Scottish highlands, the Forest of Dean or the New Forest in much the same way as Native North Americans regard the Indian Reservations?

Summer passed and the wheat ripened in the fields. My days were spent playing with Ruth the farmyard Collie, crawling through the fields in search of mice and lifting rocks in streams to seek out the innumerable tiny forms of life that dwelt there. Though perhaps unlike city dwelling children, I made no attempt to remove such creatures or disturb their habitats, for Plenty had instilled in me the same profound respect for all forms of life she herself possessed. And as the time for attendance at the Frome *Schoolarse* drew near, I played all the more intensely, somehow conscious that my life was about to change for ever and soon all this would be lost to me. As the autumn days shortened and the summer sun made her last stand against winter I commenced my formal education.

Were this a piece of fiction and not a true reminiscence, you might expect me to contrast my happy and successful learning amongst the dryads with profound unhappiness and painful experiences at school. It was not so. I remember the first day well, the playground a sea of nervous boys and girls tearfully clinging to the hands of their mothers, sucking thumbs and gripping, pleadingly, onto coattails. For my part, when that first bell rang, sounding the beginning of the end of my childhood, I simply turned to Persephone, said "Bye," and, in my newly purchased short grey trousers, ran in through the entrance marked 'girls.' I have no recollection as to when the difference was explained to me, nor the proper procedure.

Each day as I rushed out of the *Schoolarse* to Persephone I related unending tales of childish confrontations won, information gleaned and new skills acquired. It took just a few weeks before I said to her, "Persephone," (for I never used anything but her first name when addressing her since no one had ever told me to do otherwise), "can we go to Frome on Saturday to join t'library?" And from that day onwards the ancient farmhouse began to be filled with printed materials such as it had never experienced before.

When the leaves of autumn finally changed from a glorious profusion of colour to fall in crisp, lifeless brown to the ground, the dryads prepared first the trees then themselves for the long sleep of winter. By Mourning Moon our nocturnal visits to the forest ceased altogether and we focussed our attention on the coming of Yule.

I first noticed my grandfather's overnight absences following the beginning of the new Gregorian year. There was something about the routine into which the house had fallen in order for me to get to school on time that made the absence of any member of the family particularly obvious. And while my own nocturnal visits to the forest were now confined to the weekends, William's weeknight visits increased in both number and duration until his absences from the breakfast table were more frequent than his attendances.

It was following one of these overnight absences that William returned to the farmhouse to announce that 'Th' Dryads er sayin' that th' 'umans 'as declared war on th' trees.' Later a newly acquired transistor radio was to bring news of the mass application of agent orange defoliant across large areas of southeast Asia. William fully understood the purpose of its application in the context of the Vietnam war. But as he put it, "'How we'm spos'd t'explain t' th'Dryads why th'trees has to be killed fer 'uman to make war on 'uman?" As far as the Dryads were concerned, 1971 marked the declaration of all-out war. Inevitably there would be a response. It was to be more subtle and far more devastating than any of us could possibly have imagined.

My daily departure from the farmhouse for the purposes of formal education had left Persephone with reduced occupation and increased free time. Parallel to this ran her recovery from her husband's desertion and a gradual increase in sexual frustration that such an absence was bound to engender. Of course, if I had been raised in a Christian or even simply a more traditional English mode of upbringing, the recognition that my mother even possessed a sexuality of her own would have been, if not beyond my awareness, then certainly taboo as a topic of exploration even all these years later. As it was, a pre-Wiccan upbringing such as mine and one that took place in proximity to nature rendered my approach to the subject quite different from the norm of even those sexually liberated days of the 1970s.

Although it seemed insignificant to me at the time, there were increasing numbers of weeks when Persephone would find some excuse to ask Plenty to take me to school on market days. On such occasions she perhaps surmised, and rightly so, that her mother-in-law would be inclined to combine the discharge of this responsibility with a chance to visit the market and an opportunity for more social interaction than might otherwise have been possible. Did it occur to Plenty that her absence from the farmhouse would create opportunity for Persephone to enliven her former inclinations towards William? I surely think it must have done. Perhaps she considered this preferable to the potential alternative of Persephone's forming an attachment outside the immediate community with the increased likelihood of her and my departure from the farm that this would engender. Perhaps she simply accepted what she regarded as inevitable with the best grace she could muster. I will never know, for such matters were never discussed with me. Nevertheless, in 1972, at the feast of Brigid (which some covens will know by the alternative name Imbolc) Persephone announced her second pregnancy.

Superficially at least this was greeted warmly by both the Coven and the farm house community. I was nine years of age and a Wiccan. I had a comprehensive understanding of the physiology of reproduction but a total absence of understanding of its emotional implications. Do I recall a gradual waning of Plenty's astral body in those days, or have I simply superimposed such a construction on my original memories? I cannot say for certain. Either way it is my honest recollection that the joyful and energised being whom I remember from the earlier years of my childhood seemed slowly to slip away that solstice, such that by the end of Willow she had become silent and reclusive. On those market days she accompanied me to school, I would hold her tightly by the hand as we waited for the bus, not as a result of any childhood insecurity arising from her mood, but as offering the most direct method for me to connect with her and attempt to replenish her energy.

William had been prone to spending increasingly lengthy periods in the forest over the first half of that year in particular, even prior to the awakening of the dryads and the trees from their winter sleep. From the occasions on which I had accompanied him I knew this was because he was struggling increasingly with the unremitting energy demands of fighting Dutch elm disease and caring for the dryads rendered homeless and friendless by the innumerable deaths. Looking back he knew, and I think I knew, that he was fighting a battle he could not win. This, however, was no impediment to his absolute commitment to that battle on behalf of the trees. But it seemed that each time we strode into the forest by moonlight the air of death around us grew thicker, the silent mourning of the dryads for their lost children more pitiful and his own anger less concealed.

That last night, the night of Litha 1972, we walked into the forest together once more. By now far more of the elms were dead than alive, standing brittle and bare, epitaphs to their own passing. Once again I watched him kneel naked in the centre of the clearing, more dryads around him that I had ever witnessed before. In incandescent rage he beat his fists down upon the ground, all but shaking the roots of the trees about him, screaming his anger to the moon and the stars and to Abnoba and Druantia. I stood back, as he had bade me do, unable to enter into this explosion of raw, undulating energy, this anguished aphorism at his own powerlessness to prevent the inevitable. I grew older that night, older beyond my years, older than anyone had a right to expect of me.

As his passion finally subsided, and with the circle of dryads looking on in their universal and perpetual silence, he bade me kneel with him. There, that midsummer night he bestowed two gifts upon me, one verbal, one written. And surely, if it had been within my power, I would have rejected both.

He spoke to me in perfect educated English that night, such as I had never heard him employ before. I looked up into his face, still reddened and tear-stained from his outburst, and saw such love in his eyes. "'It is time for you to understand," he started, then faltered. Drawing a deep breath, he continued, "It is time for you to understand that the relationship between us is not what you understand it to be. You call me grandfather, but I am not your grandfather. I am your father. The man you knew as your father, my son Alan, is only your brother. He and your mother made a bad match from the start. As far as she was concerned the marriage was only ever a compromise. She used to bait him, enrage him unnecessarily. On that final occasion just before your fifth birthday she went too far and told him that she and I had become lovers immediately after she moved in with us. He left the next morning with the travellers and we have heard nothing from him since."

William went on to tell me he had provided for a future for me. I was to complete my local school education, proceed to Marlborough College and to Edinburgh University's School of

Forestry. From there I would know the road forward, drawing on my shamanic training and the particular propensity he had taught me for communicating with the dryads. My training would, over the coming years, be continued under the tutelage of D____ K____ who has asked not to be named in this manuscript.

"I have to tell you," he continued, "how this world will fare. The dryads have shared with me their deep regret for the war the humans have initiated, and how they will respond. Their plan is immaculate." I remember his use of that word in particular. It was so uncharacteristic of the side of himself that William had chosen not to reveal to me until now, and represented an aspect of his persona that had hitherto been completely unknown to me. "They will do absolutely nothing," he said, "for they need do nothing. They will simply withdraw their resistance to man's destructive force. This alone will hasten humanity's inexorable self-destruction, for as the dryads simply stand back the rate deforestation of the planet will accelerate. The dryads know the resultant de-oxygenation would kill all of us long before it killed all of them; and that though their numbers would be much depleted, the final self-eradication of humanity would create a world in which planetary recovery could take place."

William's second legacy was written, though not in his own hand, for he had never felt the need to master the written word. As we knelt together in the midsummer moonlight that filtered through the trees he handed me a document, drawn by a solicitor in Bristol, signed by himself and Plenty and witnessed by the High Priestess of the Frome Coven. It attested to their transfer of ownership of the farm and all their property to me. This I received in silence, understanding the facts he was telling me but uncomprehending of their import.

He stood, drawing me up with him and put his arms around me for the last time. Finally, in silence he turned me around. I took one last look at him and at the circle of dryads then I walked away. I never saw him again.

I wish I was able to report that during the intervening years the dryads had decided to declare a truce with humanity and attempt the rebuilding of the planet. Regrettably, to the best of my knowledge, they have not, and I watch with increasing concern as year by year our species races towards wanton self-destruction by the felling of countless acres of forest, now unrestrained by dryadic energy that might otherwise have saved it.

William has left to me, and to many others like me, the legacy of the education of our race in what we are doing to ourselves and to the planet. I discharge this responsibility with a little more hope than he was finally able to muster as to the possibility of reversing our self-destruction. Perhaps during my more emotionally elated times I even dare to hope that one day the dryads will again re-join their efforts with us in this work of healing, now that some of us have finally become more enlightened. I do not think William would have minded. After all, my paternal grandfather was an English shaman with a profound connection to the dryads.

16   The Rational Choice

Joshua's father had started the joinery shop all those years ago. He'd opened it in a little back street workshop that no one else had wanted. Because of the years of neglect the place had suffered, Davidson was able to negotiate a reduced rent. It had taken him and his fiancée weeks to prepare the ramshackle rooms, clearing the rubbish that had piled up over years of neglect and letting the light in for the first time in decades. By the time they were ready to open the doors for business, there was no one in town that was unaware of the work that the young couple had put in and they were universally wished well. It came as no surprise to any of their neighbours when the business prospered, for the young couple were well known for their deeply held values of hard work, a desire for security and a true religious commitment.

Of course, given that religious commitment, numerous eyebrows were raised when rumours began to spread that Davidson's fiancée had fallen pregnant. When that coincided with an extended business trip, many put two and two together and the gossiping became rife. But when the young couple returned home married, with a new baby son in arms, the carrion gossips found richer fare upon which to feast, and the apparent misdemeanour was soon forgotten.

Davidson's joinery shop prospered over the years as his family grew. The man took pride in the quality of his work and the home and security he was providing for his wife and children. That first boy – Joshua – was the light of his life. He spent virtually all his free waking hours watching and working with Davidson, the skills of the craft and his father's values slowly infusing his personality.

Those that met the boy recognised something unusual about him – a certain maturity that was uncommon for a child of

115

his age; an 'old soul' someone had called him once, and somehow it seemed an appropriate label. Joshua himself sensed something different about himself... something difficult to articulate... an awareness, or perhaps a 'calling' that abided in his soul, just out of the reach of consciousness.

As the business expanded, Davidson took on assistants until the joinery shop was full, humming with activity as it turned out window frames and tables, doors and carvings. At the end of the working day, after returning from school, Joshua would take the broom from the back of the shop and sweep the chippings and sawdust away from the work areas. He studied the work of the assistants carefully, silently observing the strengths and weaknesses of each, seeing how every man's personality was reflected into his workmanship. Here was one who was impatient. His dovetails were inaccurate, and it was obvious to Joshua that the windows he created would rot quickly, as water seeped into the joints. He knew his father would not retain the services of that individual for long. Here were the intricate carvings of another upon a lintel. The customer had neither asked nor paid for such loving work, and Joshua knew the carver would have lavished such attention in his own time, not the shop's. He noted mentally that this assistant would go far. Thus as the years passed, Joshua's knowledge of the wood working industry and of the state of men's souls deepened and matured.

Eventually, The day came when he finished school and, as all the family had assumed, joined his father in the workshop. It was Davidson's proudest moment when he painted the words 'and Son' at the end of the sign that hung over the doorway.

Around the dinner table each evening the parents and their children would talk over the day's events. The conversation would consistently gravitate to the same two subjects – the success of the joinery shop with the security and material wealth it had brought them all, and the deep spiritual commitment that each member of the family shared. This was a family that worked hard for what it had and knew it was blessed.

The years rolled on. Joshua found himself in his twenties, the age that all children yearn to attain, yet during childhood can barely conceive they will ever reach. Then later, as each of his brothers had finished school, his father had initiated them into the family business one by one. 'And son' had long been replaced by 'And sons' over the door of the workshop, which itself had now been expanded, to encompass the premises on each side of it as they had fallen vacant over the years.

At the end of the working day on which his youngest brother had been taken into the business, Joshua stood alone in the joinery shop and gazed around him. He thought of his childhood years when he had loved to sweep up the chippings and sawdust. He thought of his growing awareness in his early teens of the moral condition of men's hearts, when he had learned to discern the state of a man's soul through the attitudes he presented to the world. He thought of his own growing awareness of the fact that there might soon be more to his life than simply running the successful business that he, his father and his brothers had laboured to create. That which had lain latent in his soul until the appointed time, now began to rise to the surface. As he stood alone that evening in the silence of the workshop, he saw a vision of two potential futures.

On the one hand, he could expect to continue as he was, satisfying the very real and natural urges to fall in love and father a family of his own, to enjoy material wealth and provide security for himself and his loved ones. On the other hand, he sensed some sort of a calling to a different kind of labour. It was as though during the years that the skills of his hands had developed, so too an analogous set of skills had been developing in his soul. He had laboured to create timber products and carvings all through his life. Now, something inside himself said to him that if he chose to accept it, a new commission would arise – that of carving revelation and truth into the souls of men. Troubled, he returned home and was silent at the dinner table that evening, letting his family's conversation and joyful laughter wash over him.

The visions did not stop. In fact they intensified. As the weeks rolled into months and then into years, so the representations of the two alternative futures grew. More clearly now, he saw one scenario of material wealth and security as he and his brothers laboured to perfect the work that his father had started. In his mind's eye he saw himself meeting the girl of his dreams, marrying and bringing a family of his own into the world. He saw growth in the business. He saw himself and his brothers prospering, expanding the joinery shop, opening new branches in other towns, becoming a dominant commercial force in the province.

At other times he saw himself turning the key in the lock of the joinery shop for the last time, turning to his assembled brothers and hugging them one by one. He then saw himself walking away as his siblings stood shaking their heads in silent confusion. In this vision of the future his representation of what happened next was cloudy. But he could not get away from the sense of calling he carried as the end of his twenties drew inexorably closer. He visualised, in some inexpressible fashion, that many would be blessed if he were to heed the calling. He saw crowds before him, as he felt the words of truth lodge themselves in his mind just at the moment he needed to speak them. He saw the healing of souls and of bodies. He saw his own awareness of spiritual truth and the word of life reaching out to those who were ready to hear. But he saw also darkness and sadness to be passed through. Then he saw beyond the darkness into a future in which the souls of countless numbers would be touched. He would shake himself from the trance and wonder if all this amounted to no more than self-inflated daydreaming. "Delusions of grandeur," he would say to himself on such occasions, and his mind would revert to the joinery shop and the next day's work schedule. In his saner moments he knew that the rational choice would be to stick with his brothers in the business and enjoy a life of comfort and security.

As Joshua's thirtieth birthday approached, the family planned a surprise party for him. He was aware that the coming of the change of decade was something of a watershed; that if he were going to act on the vision it would have to be soon or never. As the months before that birthday diminished into weeks and finally into days, Joshua became more and more focused on the decision that lay before him. 'There's nothing wrong with being a joiner,' he thought to himself. 'Plenty of upright spiritual people are respectable artisans, serving man honestly with their hands and serving God faithfully in their hearts.' Thus he would reason, until the vision of the Calling came upon him once more, and he was swept away into the spirit on a wave of awareness of what he was being asked to do.

By the time his birthday actually arrived, someone had long since let the secret of the surprise party slip, and Joshua was well forewarned. He took the event in the spirit in which it was meant though, playing along as if he knew nothing about it. As the celebrations extended into the evening, and the music and the wine flowed, Joshua became keenly aware of the life of ease that could be his. He looked around at his friends and neighbours dancing and laughing, and the several attractive young women that his brothers had invited with a view to one of them catching his eye.

Joshua made his choice that night.

Unexpectedly, Davidson took the opportunity of the evening's gathering to announce his own retirement and the gifting of the business to his sons. The old man expressed supreme confidence that Joshua would rise to the challenge of managerial control and that the new responsibility would be good for him. And as he delivered his speech, Davidson looked proudly on the young man, whom he had every confidence would continue to grow in personality and in spirituality.

The brothers never did change the sign that hung over the doorway. For within a year of the old man's retirement, Joshua had married and fathered a son. As everyone anticipated, the business prospered under his management. His brothers continued to work with him and there was peace and harmony in the workshop. As the years rolled by, gradually Joshua's visions of the alternative life he might have led waned, until he was troubled by them only at night, and then infrequently. The years of prosperity rolled on until the time for handing over the business to his own son arrived. It was more than coincidence that he too made the handover speech on the evening of his son's thirtieth birthday.

Joshua bought a retirement villa overlooking lake Galilee. Friends who visited him there were apt to notice a certain sense of unfulfilment about him that slid rapidly into early onset dementia. Sadly, he died all too soon, drowned in the lake. It was rumoured that he had tried to walk over the water one evening to dine with his friends.

17   The Power Giver

"What do you crave most at this moment?" I ask, my voice barely audible in the falling twilight.

The Returner stands before me, dishevelled, weary. His long grey beard is unkempt, his hands are calloused from a lifetime of physical labour. He looks at me momentarily, considering his answer carefully. "Power," he replies, making no attempt to embellish the response with implausible justifications. Clearly, this man is a Truth Speaker.

I knew the answer already, of course. Long, long ago I learned to read the hearts of The Returners by looking into their eyes. Some might make a feeble attempt to resist me, hoping I see nothing but my own reflection when I peer into their souls. None succeed. Always, I win. Always, I see the visions of frustration etched on their irises. For they have done battle with The Fire and with The Ice, The Returners. And they have lost.

Thus, they have had to suppress their weariness, their howling, screaming exhaustion a little longer as they approach me once more. For they know and I know it is I alone who can offer them The Change they seek. For this is Journey's End and there is no other to whom they can turn. I am The Gate Keeper. I hold the only Key to the Change. And they know that without The Change they cannot have The Power they crave.

Once I sought to influence their use of The Power. I tried to tell them that it held great danger, that it needed to be exercised with utmost care. But that was long, long ago. Now I have acknowledged that once I grant The Change I can exercise no further influence over how The Power is utilised. Some of The Returners will use The Power to become enlightened, bringing warmth and illumination to those they love. Sadly, others – the Unwise Ones – will misuse The Power. These are they that will burn and be burned.

But I cannot fool myself, for I am answerable to a Higher Authority. So long as the Returners furnish me with The Note I have no right to withhold The Change.

As I look into the eyes of the one who stands before me now, I know that this time there is no risk. He will use The Power wisely. He has lived long and understands its dangers. And yes, he is indeed holding The Note in his outstretched hand. I take it and study it closely. The illustrations are exquisite. The signature is one with which I am familiar and clearly genuine. The Note contains a Promise which I evaluate carefully, for one cannot be too sure of Promises. But in this case I believe I can trust the Signatory to keep the Promise. I therefore accept The Note and place in The Returner's outstretched palm the Five Golden Coins that are The Change that will give him The Power.

He looks at me with gratitude and relief. "Sorry," I hear myself saying, "I should have mentioned when you arrived here at Journey's End Holiday Park that the meters in the caravans take only one pound coins."

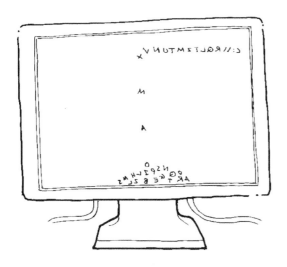

18   In Memory of the Tishbite

He told me that the words never started as words. They came first as sooty wisps of thought, dancing upwards from a primeval camp fire at dusk; movements that he could see better out of the corner of his eye. If he turned to face them head on, they would evaporate into the twilight of the then-time before he had a chance to focus and force them to tell him their story. He never knew exactly how they would coalesce before they appeared in front of him on the page, when it was too late to change the way they had fashioned themselves. Maybe it had always been this way for him – crystallising the silent spectres from the periphery of his vision, the happenings on the event horizon of his awareness. Back in time and space he eventually learned how to catch hold of the ghosts and pin them to the paper, where they finally consented to be subjugated to just a little discipline. Harsh taskmaster that he was, he would shake them awake into the now-time, make them rub the sleep from their eyes and drive them in punishing early morning workouts until finally they acquiesced to become phrases and sentences, bursting with euphoria and pathos; ectoplasmic incoherence crystallised.

Once they became his to control as he chose, he loved to play with the words – to dance hand in hand with them, hurling them around the dancehall to the jive tunes of his own inner jazz band until, breathless and giddy, complex philosophies juxtaposed themselves against giggles of frivolity. This was the way he extemporised his more elegant kind of music out of the form and structure that leading edge writers like to think it's cool to disdain.

It was this that reassured him in the afraid times that he was an artist. He didn't sketch and he didn't draw, he didn't mix palettes of paint and he didn't brush oil on canvas. It was in the cadences and clauses and in the sheer living movement of metaphor that he sculpted. Here he would rub down the rusty chassis of worn out realities and respray them with his own startling kind of awareness. Just when you thought he was going to back some clichéd old runabout out of the garage of his imagination, he'd catch you out with a whole tool bag of modifications and innovations, tuning up the clapped out characters and revving the engine of the story into a Grand Prix version that was all of his own making.

Like others that walked the path before him he was a tortured soul; terrified when he wrote that it wouldn't be good enough to be real art; terrified when he didn't write that the words, even if he considered them worthless, would simply stop appearing. And for this he hated himself at times. Which artist doesn't? Oh, he threw a mantle of flippancy over the hatred that was woven just closely enough to fool the superficial majority. But the hatred was there, nevertheless. He hated that he needed to feel safe and that he gravitated to that which spoke soothingly into his turbulence.

Mostly, he knew that that safety was meaningless. It never hid from him for long that he was a driver in an otherwise empty car, clinging in terror to the seat belt as it flew off the edge of the cliffs of confidence into the deoxygenated atmosphere of his own insecurity. Then he would plummet downwards, falling like some cartoon stooge, falling for eternity.

Yet when eternity was over, somehow he always landed right way up, and he would emerge from the crisis, his mind crammed full of ideas that crawled over each other like bees fleeing a burning hive, squiggles of incomprehension that surged into representations of other realities, other ways of looking at the world that you never saw before, yet which you knew you'd always known when he showed them to you.

And when the critics sprayed their graffiti over the news print, in his own inimitable way he would seize their spray cans and overwrite the skate park walls of public acclamation with the dismissive metaphors of insightfulness that only he could form, leading them towards the light of his own reality. He took the very praise they heaped upon his work and twisted it, like a fairground clown bending balloons, into caricatures of their own uneasiness that left them feeling faintly ridiculous for ever needing to give voice to their praises in the first place.

Then he'd pick up his pen again, and the letters would ooze seductively down the side of the hive to collect in pools of sweet, malleable, word craft written in honey: an inspired poem here, an insightful story there, a piece of prose so beautiful in its constitution that it froze your mid-sentence breath into ice statues of awakened realisation.

That was why he was working, always working, polishing the words and making them shine until he could see his own essence reflected in them. Only then were they good enough to ship out in wooden crates by the thousand to let the world use as mirrors to its soul.

Before he left, he asked me, "What shall I do for you before I am taken away from you?"

I answered, "My Father, let a double portion of your spirit be upon me."

That was fifteen years ago. I still have the mantle. But I have not struck Jordan with it. Who would dare?

19   Vile Body

Madeleine can't stop crying. She's always like this when she's about to kill one of her children. The pain she feels is indescribable but the need for termination of imperfect progeny is beyond dispute. It was Daddy, dear, dear Daddy who taught her that such aberrations must be eradicated as soon as discovered. He also taught her that it is kinder if this is done quickly.

Each time she gives birth, Madeleine is hopeful for her new child. At first she looks upon it with a radiant, all pervading love. So overwhelmed is she by the thought that this independent life came from inside herself, that she is incapable of seeing any imperfection. She engages with the new infant; looks at it this way and that; talks to it incessantly; works with dedication on its development. Then, as novelty yields to familiarity, she notices some minor deformity. Initially she convinces herself that this is unimportant; that the child will develop strong and healthy regardless and will outgrow such an insignificant imperfection of, perhaps, skeletal structure or sense.

Yet as each child reaches that point of adolescent detachment and begins to grow away from her, out of her control (and somehow, it is always at the end of chapter VI that this happens), she is forced to acknowledge that yes, this child, too, is deformed.

Always it ends the same. Always there must be cleansing. Always there must be death.

Madeleine has experimented with many forms of extermination over the years; death by submersion has too often failed to obscure completely; death by the blade can always be reversed. No, it has long since been established that there is only one form of eradication open to a loving parent such as herself who seeks true perfection – and that is death by fire. Why did it take her so long to realise this when it was Daddy himself that had shown her it was so all those years ago?

Today is Maddie's seventh birthday. She is playing with her babies in the corner of her bedroom: Suzy-Jane and Lady Sarah, Ragged Julie and Baby Mary, Teddy and Barbie who must never be parted. Maddie loves her babies. She wants for them to love her back. They want so much to show her they love her too but they cannot move. Maddie wants her babies to move but she cannot make them move.

Now comes the shadow; a darkness, creeping over her from behind, so slowly that at first she barely notices. For Maddie is too busy loving her babies: Suzy-Jane and Lady Sarah, Ragged Julie and Baby Mary, Teddy and Barbie who must never be parted. The shadow spreads until she and they are covered. They can all hear it breathing behind them.

Now the shadow speaks. "It is time Madeleine. When I was a child I thought as a child, I spoke as a child. But when I became a man I put away childish things." Maddie wants to argue, but she cannot make herself argue. Suzy-Jane and Lady Sarah, Ragged Julie and Baby Mary, Teddy and Barbie who must never be parted all want to argue but they cannot argue.

And so, one still summer evening, Madeleine descends the fire escape from her second floor Camden Lock apartment to the communal back garden, where the area allocated to her flat is the one furthest from the converted house. Other allocated spaces indicate the leisure proclivities of the tenants – a climbing frame here, neat rows of Brussels sprouts and lettuces there – but Madeleine's territory is different. It is overgrown with savannah length grass, all except for a trampled path that leads from the broken wicket gate to the centre of the plot. There stands an ancient brazier, its bright red paint almost entirely peeled away by rust.

From the front pocket of Madeleine's apron protrudes a bottle of barbeque lighter fluid, and hidden further down there is a box of matches. In her right hand she carries one of her precious children; in her left is its identical twin, a carbon copy. She lowers one bunioned foot in front of the other down the fire escape steps, gripping her children tightly. As a result she is unable to use the handrail to steady herself. Yet she will not risk loosening her grip on them, lest they blow away and their imperfection be scattered to the winds. She reaches the ground successfully, her face reddened with rosacea and effort. Morbid obesity has long since caused her features to recede into the drooping flesh of her face. Madeleine's only concessions to femininity are an auburn Henna rinse now six weeks old and bright red, though terminally chewed, fingernails.

'And the Lord said unto Abraham, Take now thy son, thine only son Isaac, whom thou lovest, and offer him for a burnt offering upon the alter I shall show thee.'

Suzy-Jane and Lady Sarah, Ragged Julie and Baby Mary, Teddy and Barbie who must never be parted look at her, pleading for Maddie to save them, but she cannot save them.

"Put away thy childish things, Madeleine," says the voice. "Take now thy babies whom thou lovest and offer them for a burnt offering upon the alter I shall show thee." They want to move but they cannot move, Suzy-Jane and Lady Sarah, Ragged Julie and Baby Mary, Teddy and Barbie who must never be parted. Maddie wants to move and she can move but only as the voice tells her to move. "Take now thy babies Madeleine." She picks up her babies. Baby Mary squeaks and blinks her eyes sadly. Barbie is in her evening dress. Suzy-Jane is sullen, silent.

"Turn around, Madeleine."

Maddie obeys; with her babies in her arms she turns towards the shadow that is a raven with white eyes. It leads her by its will alone. Maddie wants to not move but she cannot not move. The shadow is the raven with white eyes. It leads her into the back garden of the Victorian Vicarage in Putney where it has cleared a space. In the space stands a brazier that is painted bright red. Together they stand by the brazier and peer down inside. Maddie and the raven with white eyes and Suzy-Jane and Lady Sarah, Ragged Julie and Baby Mary, and Teddy and Barbie who must never be parted. There is a fire of charcoal burning steadily at the bottom. The raven with white eyes looks at Maddie. The babies want to move, but they cannot move. Maddie holds out her arms to the raven. Her babies quiver in her hands. The raven leads her with his white eyes to the fire. Maddie turns to face the fire, arms still outstretched.

Madeleine proceeds towards the execution chamber. She arrives, peers down into the altar at the ashes that remain from previous sacrifices, then gently lays the sheets of these two most recent progenies in the bottom of the brazier. She sprinkles lighter fluid sparingly upon the pages, strikes a match and drops it onto her children. They want to move but they cannot move, Madeleine's children. Madeleine is quite certain that she sees in them, in their silence and passivity, a true understanding of why this must be. And now, though her heart weeps and her soul screams, her eyes remain dry.

As she watches the flames rise from the funeral pyre she mumbles the old, old incantation that she has spoken across so many cremations (she would much prefer that Daddy said these words but recognises that, sadly, since the stroke he is incapable of descending the stairs):

"Ashes to ashes, dust to dust; in sure and certain hope of the Resurrection to eternal life, through our Lord Jesus Christ; who shall change our vile body, that it may be like unto his glorious body, according to the mighty working, whereby he is able to subdue all things to himself."

She pronounces life extinguished at exactly 9.47 pm; with the smoke still rising from the altar of appeasement, she turns her back.

Madeleine reaches the bottom of the fire escape steps and looks up to her flat. She grips the iron handrail and commences the Annapurnian ascent.

"Vile Body," she mutters, "… vile body… change to glorious body… subdue all things… subdue all things." As her feet ascend, her spirit, too, begins to rise. Now it is time to work. With each elevating step she enters further into trance wherein she knows from long experience that the act of procreation will be perpetrated upon her by the Holy Spirit. At these moments she likes to think of the Virgin Mary. Her dearest dream is that one day all generations will also call Madeleine blessed. By the time she reaches the top of the fire escape the Shadow of the Holy Spirit has covered her and ethereal impregnation is complete. Madeleine has conceived.

The morning sun falls upon a sleeping form; respiration is deep and regular. Madeleine has worked and dreamed and woken; worked and dreamed and woken in a cycle that is now so familiar to her as to be beyond comment. The Shadow of the Holy Spirit does not cover her every night, but each night that He does, the pattern is the same. Six chapters; six periods of sleep; six awakenings.

Madeleine never gets to Chapter VII.

Her body is sprawled across the wheel-back chair with the missing spoke that stands in front of the old pine kitchen table. These, together with the brazier, she liberated from the Victorian Vicarage near Putney Bridge years ago.

Upon the table stands an old Brother typewriter, still functioning, though the bottom part of the 'e' key has worn away, so that Madeleine's 'e's are left hovering above the words in which they appear like rows of little space invaders. To the right of the typewriter stand three piles of paper; one pile of top copies, one of carbon sheets and one of second copies. By working through the night Madeleine has given birth to another child, this one named 'Ezmeralda's Folly.' She is particularly proud of this mis-spelling of 'Esmeralda,' for it is central to the plot in which the heiress is disinherited by virtue of her inability to prove her identity with legal documentation. Madeleine has high hopes for this child: at this moment it appears to her to be quite perfect.

"Open," says the raven with white eyes. Maddie wants to not move but she cannot not move. She opens her hands. They want to not fall, Suzy-Jane and Lady Sarah, Ragged Julie and Baby Mary, Teddy and Barbie who must never be parted. They want so much to not die, but they cannot not die.

"Ashes to ashes, dust to dust," says the raven with white eyes. "He will change our vile body that it may be like unto his glorious body, Madeleine."

The raven leads Maddie back to her bedroom by its will. "Open," says the raven with white eyes. Maddie wants so much to not open, but she cannot not open. Maddie is Suzy-Jane and she is Lady Sarah and she is Ragged Julie and she is Baby Mary and Maddie is Teddy and Barbie who have been parted. Maddie so wants not to be seven years old but she cannot not be seven years old and Madeleine is burning in the fire.

Now she takes dear Daddy his early morning tea. As she enters the room and sees he is already in his chair by the window, dressed in the black shirt and dog collar of his working years, she smiles a benevolent smile at him. Dear Daddy who has taught and given her so much, and now is in so much need of her care; dear, dear Daddy who, following the strokes, is blind (though she has taken steps to preserve his eyes, lest his sight should one day miraculously return) and can barely move on his own; how she loves him. She looks at him with concern. It is not the body odour that bothers her. She would never, never mention this to him – it is simply not the proper place of a loving daughter to discuss such matters with her elderly father. Her concern is that he seems emaciated, bony… perhaps one might even say skeletal. What is she to do? It is so long since he has been willing to take sustenance. She puts the cup and saucer down on the window ledge where dear blind Daddy could reach it if he were minded to, takes away the cold one and tip toes out of the room so as not to disturb him.

She returns to her typing table and looks down upon her new born child. She seats herself once more, slides the typewriter further away from her to make space and reaches for the carbon copy of the manuscript. She hesitates, stops and instead draws to her the top copy. This child will be given the very best possible chance of life. Madeleine studies the title page carefully. 'Ezmerelda's Folly,' it reads. 'By Madeleine.' There is no surname. 'If Michelangelo can be Michelangelo, if Lassie can be Lassie,' she reasons, 'then Madeleine can be Madeleine.'

As she turns over the title page her heart rate rises, for she knows that confrontation follows. Confrontation is good in a novel, of course, even essential. However, this is the confrontation not of content, but of structure.

The problem leers up at her, taunting her with its implications. Never has an author been so scared of two words: Chapter VII. Why would Madeleine be intimidated by such an innocuous, commonplace phrase, you ask? The answer is simple. Chapter I itself is complete, perfect. Chapter two sleeps safely beneath it. But Chapter I and Chapter II imply Chapter III and Chapter IV, and further Roman numerals potentially rising to untold combinations until the magnum opus finally reaches that elusive, longed for epitaph: *finis.*

Madeleine has never legitimately written *finis* at the end of a work by cause of the fact that she has never actually finished a work. Frequently she has typed *finis* onto pure, clean sheets of paper, simply to fantasise over how it would feel to be able to add it without guilt to one of her manuscripts.

She is interrupted by the rattle of the letter box. Madeleine detests the intrusion of the outside world. Indeed, she has long since arranged bill payment by direct debit, registered with the Postal Preference Service and posted a notice outside the door threatening would-be depositors of unsolicited junk mail with terrifying consequences. Madeleine therefore wonders what possible reason there is for an item to pass through the letter box.

She rises once more from the chair and makes her way to the front door where a DL sized brown envelope lies face down upon the floor. She retrieves it with her grabber, lifts it to reading distance. The words 'Camden Borough Council' stare accusingly at her. She hesitates, nervous as to what it might contain, dismisses a fleeting thought that it should be read in front of Daddy, then brazenly tears it open. A planning application; the ground floor of her building is to be turned into a bookshop; there is a date by which she must object should she wish to do so.

Madeleine collapses involuntarily into the wheel-back chair, causing a second spoke to snap.

She can barely contemplate the number of imperfect children this implies… and children not her own, at that. It is one thing to tolerate imperfection in one's own offspring, it is quite another to bear such deficiencies in the bastard progeny of other so-called authors in virtually limitless numbers; and all without the possibility of termination. What is worse is that it is quite possible that one or more of these children may have been permitted to live beyond chapter seven.

Madeleine is now entirely incapable of expressing herself coherently, and the possibility of writing anything meaningful is out of the question. She is forced to tell dear Daddy. So shocked is he that he is completely unable to respond; his cups of tea accumulate on the window ledge, growing cold and filmy.

Novel writing is postponed in favour of daily letter writing. Each letter has required a difficult trip down the fire escape to the post office during which it has been impossible for her to ignore the preparatory work that has already commenced on the ground floor of her building. Official responses initially poured through the letter box, assuring her that her correspondence would be taken into account; that her views were important. But as the pile of carbon copies of her own letters grows higher on the writing table, gradually the inbound responses become less frequent and eventually cease entirely.

Some weeks later, a final brown envelope arrives. Once again the grabber is employed, the envelope torn open. Planning approval has been granted for a Cornerstone's Bookshop.

Later – though she cannot say how much later – she awakes to find herself on the floor still clutching the letter. She struggles to a seated position with a single thought on her mind: when diplomacy has failed there is but one option left to righteous nations. She thinks of dear Mr Churchill and the wonderful Dame Margaret. She visualises herself donning a tin hat to man the barricades of Camden Lock with an Enfield Number 4 rifle. The deformed children will not, positively *not*, be allowed to live here in her building. Madeleine is going to war.

It appears she has some weeks before the shop opens. She considers leafleting the neighbourhood; writing to her MP (she thinks she probably has one); standing in the doorway to prevent public entry. She dismisses such strategies as too ineffectual, for she is but one woman, and one life is all she has. One life is all… but wait a moment. Isn't that a quotation? Yes… yes… it's coming back to her now. 'One life is all we have and we live it as we believe in living it.' Joan of Arc! The quotation is from Joan of Arc! And now there are more … 'I am not afraid. I was born to do this!' Yes, oh yes! At last Madeleine understands what her life has been for! Now she sees the purpose of her training with fire at dear Daddy's hands under the Holy Spirit's guidance! Dear St Joan was called at France's moment of need to rid the country of God's enemies. And in just the same way it falls to her, St Madeleine of

Putney to rid Camden Lock of the Blasphemers and their Bastard Malformed Children!

St Madeleine bursts through the door into dear Daddy's bedroom, oblivious to the possibility that he might be performing devotionals or addressing *Personal Needs*. But no, she is fortunate for he is still sitting as he always does, facing the window, dressed in the black suit, black shirt and dog collar, bony hands still holding onto the arms of the chair. In mounting excitement she explains the vision of the Holy Spirit that has come upon her to make her a saint and how he, dear Daddy, must help her, for it is he that taught her the use of fire and this is therefore their Joint Work.

It is morning. The sun has risen reluctantly. It wanted to not rise but it could not not rise. Madeleine is sitting in the corner of her room. She wants to play with her babies but she cannot play with her babies, for Suzy-Jane and Lady Sarah have been burned and Teddy and Barbie who must never be parted have been parted. Maddie cannot unburn Ragged Julie and Baby Mary, for their vile bodies are ashes and dust, and their eyes have melted in the fire. And she cannot bring together Teddy and Barbie, for Teddy and Barbie are too sore.

Her babies had planned a surprise breakfast for Maddie. They had set the table out yesterday on her birthday with the plastic cups ready for the pretend tea and plastic plates ready for the pretend chocolate cake. But the pretend tea has grown cold and the pretend chocolate cake is dry and bitter and though yesterday was Madeleine's seventh birthday she will never, never again let herself get to seven.

St Madeleine cannot contain her excitement during the fit out period of The Bookshop. She uses it to gather intelligence on the Enemy, to spot his weaknesses, devise the strategy that will drive him out forever. St Madeleine now spends her days sitting in the window of The Smiling Spoon Café opposite which affords her commanding views of the Enemy's progress. Binoculars and notebook have replaced typewriter and carbon paper as the tools of her trade for as long as hostilities will continue.

Now the shadow comes again; Madeleine wants to not see the shadow but she cannot not see it. The shadow that is the raven with white eyes has opened the door. It has entered the bedroom. Now it is coming closer, and Madeleine wants to move but she cannot move and the raven with white eyes is almost upon her and its shadow is covering her and she can smell its feathers and see its talons and Madeleine knows for certain that Suzy-Jane has been burned and Baby Mary's eyes have melted and Teddy and Barbie will be parted again and she wants them not to be parted because they are so very sore but they cannot not be parted because the shadow that is the raven with white eyes is coming, coming, coming.

But now the raven stops, stands in front of her and holds out something in its paw: for now the raven with white eyes has become a black dog with a white collar. And now the black dog with the white collar speaks and says "No man can be called friendless who has God and the companionship of good books. Do you know who first said that, Madeleine?" The black dog with the white collar does not wait for an answer. "It was Elizabeth Barrett Browning. And now you are seven you will read. Here, a book of quality." The black dog with the white collar turns and leaves and now the raven is gone and so is the shadow and Madeleine is glad.

The book is called *The Three Musketeers* by someone called Alexandre Dumas, pere. All that day Madeleine reads the book, chapter by chapter. She does not understand all the words and her babies are not here to explain them to her but she does not mind and she is glad to spend her not-seventh-birthday reading. And then she arrives at the end of chapter six. But when she turns the page, Madeleine carefully tears out all the remaining pages, for she can never, never reach Chapter seven because if seven comes Suzy-Jane and Lady Sarah and Ragged Julie and Baby Mary will have to be burned again and their eyes will have to melt in the fire again and poor sore Teddy and Barbie who must never be parted will be parted.

Tonight the shadow returns. As Madeleine watches the handle of the door twist round she wonders whether the shadow will be the raven with white eyes or the black dog with a white collar. But it really does not matter which it is, for the shadow sees the book and the shadow is angry that there is no chapter seven nor any pages beyond. And Madeleine wants to move as the shadow parts Teddy and Barbie who must never be parted even when she tells the shadow how very, very sore they are. And when the shadow has gone and the raven with white eyes has gone and the black dog with the white collar has gone, Madeleine knows that this is what it is like to be seven and to be grown up and that there will be more nights that the shadow will come and more night her babies will burn and more nights poor sore Teddy and Barbie will be parted.

Opening day has come. St Madeleine passes the day prayerfully, in and out of dear Daddy's room, checking she has everything she will need for tonight. Eventually, 23.00 hours arrives. St Madeleine puts dear Daddy's eyes in – she has been storing them in the jar of pickles in the kitchen cupboard for long enough now, and there will never be another moment as important as this for him to look his best. She places his overcoat about his shoulders. Finally she dons her own camouflage fatigues. Most important of all, she places in her pocket the barbeque lighter fluid and matches. She lifts dear Daddy from the chair with little effort, for he is so light now and he makes no effort to resist.

Carefully, St Madeleine descends the fire escape steps. From underneath the bottom step she retrieves an axe where she secreted it earlier in the day, then makes her way to the rear entrance of Cornerstone's. She sits dear Daddy on the ground, lays the axe momentarily to the lock then swings it back. It crashes down, splitting the wood, making the door fly back against the wall. Madeleine raises dear Daddy in her arms and strides into the Enemy camp.

The Enemy is complacent: he has left his stronghold unguarded.

Using only the light from the streetlamps at the front of the shop, St Madeleine moves forward to the till, depositing dear Daddy gently on the swivel chair behind the counter. He slumps to one side. She straightens him and pushes his left eyeball back into place, for it has worked slightly loose. The number of volumes in the Enemy camp takes her by surprise. There is no time to remove any of the Chapter VIIs and beyond that might be in some of them.

139

They will simply have to burn along with each volume's Chapters I–VI. St Madeleine sets to, sprinkling lighter fluid in a stream from the central counter to the lower shelves of 'Cookery'.

But what is this? She hears a rustling coming from 'Psychology'. St Madeleine peers round the edge of the section and can barely suppress a scream of surprise and joy. For here are Suzy-Jane and Lady Sarah, determinedly stripping Chapter VII and chapters beyond from each volume and throwing them onto a pile in the middle of the aisle. She weeps with happiness to see them, but there is no time now for a demonstrative reunion, for there is work to be done; time is short. As she climbs the stairs to 'Children's Books' she is now not in the least surprised to see Ragged Julie and Baby Mary systematically applying cigarette lighters to the volumes within their reach.

God has been good to her! He has restored her dearly beloved babies to support her in this, the hour of her calling. Now she understands why they had to be sacrificed. Dear, dear Daddy must have known all along what St Madeleine's future held and what help she would need.

Satisfied that all is ready she returns to the central counter on the ground floor for it is time to call the fire of absolution down from Heaven. With near disinterest St Madeleine notices that a crowd has begun to gather outside the front window of the bookshop. They are shouting and banging on the door, twisting the handle this way and that.

They want to break in but they cannot break in. St Madeleine wants them not to break in.

She turns her attention to dear Daddy. And what a joyful surprise! Who should be sitting on his lap but Teddy and Barbie who must never be parted. They are swinging playfully on his thighs, forcing them wide open then snapping them closed again. St Madeleine hopes they are not sore and she hopes that dear Daddy is not sore as she was once sore.

Now she begins to sing softly the old, old Pentecostal hymn. Dear Daddy never really approved of Pentecostal hymns, but this one seems so appropriate to the occasion she feels he will not mind:

Let the fire fall!

Let the fire fall!
Let the fire from Heaven fall.
We are waiting and expecting, in faith dear Lord we call.

St Madeleine lights the cleansing flame and touches it to the stream of lighter fluid that runs from the central counter to '2 for 1 Fiction'. As she stands back to watch the purifying fire spread across the Deformed Bastard Children, she sees that Suzy-Jane and Lady Sarah, Ragged Julie and Baby Mary, and Teddy and Barbie who must never be parted have formed a circle around dear Daddy. They too are singing. St Madeleine claps her hands in ecstasy! Her babies have formed themselves into her choir and are continuing with her hymn:

Let the fire fall, let the fire fall…

And look, oh, look! Look at dear Daddy! He wants to be a raven with white eyes, but he cannot be a raven with white eyes. He wants to be a black dog with a white collar but he cannot be a black dog with a white collar. He can only be the skeletal remains of a long dead, incestuous vicar with pickled eyes. He wants to not burn but he cannot not burn, for the fire has fallen from Heaven upon him. He wants to see but he cannot see, for his eyes are melting in the fire.

20   Obituary for Football

Once upon a time there was a game called football. The last game ever played was an FA cup final. It went like this:

Onto the pitch walks the referee. Everyone cheers. The referee then hands instruction manuals to the team captains.

The teams' members are puzzled, but go into conference, one at each end of the pitch.

The crowd looks on. They are puzzled too.

Then the conferring is over. Everyone returns to their positions. The excitement in the crowd gathers. The ref is about to blow his whistle when…

Another referee walks onto the pitch. No one cheers. Lots of people in the crowd start to mumble, "Get on with the game!"(at least I think that's what all those four letter words mean). The second referee hands instruction manuals to the team captains. The teams go into conference, one at each end of the pitch, for a second time.

The crowd looks on, puzzled. Again.

Then the conferring is over. Everyone returns to their positions. At last we can start the game.

Except the two refs can't decide on what the start time should be.

And the team players are starting to whisper – the rule books contain different instruction. They have different priorities. Which rules should be followed first? Which take priority?

"Oh, that's easy," say the two refs in unison. "Follow all the rules but prioritise mine first. Mine are the most important."

The players shake their heads in confusion but return to their positions. They are the best footballers in the country. That's why their teams have reached the FA Cup Final. They know their job – it's to play well for the success of their team and give the spectators a good time. So they try to satisfy the two refs and still get the job done.

Now the refs have agreed on a start time. They both look at their watches. They are about to blow their whistles in unison when...

A third ref struts onto the pitch. And guess what? He hands a third set of instructions to the captains who ... guess what? Pass them to the players, who go into a third holy huddle.

But they're used to this by now. They know the refs have the force of the rule books behind them and must be obeyed. If not, there will be sanctions. They could be banned from playing for non-compliance with the rule book.

Not to mention the publicised shame of their incompetence (though they're all competent footballers, you understand. It's just that following rule books and using the right language has little to do with footballing skill). Nevertheless, they'll do their best to comply with all the regulations in case the dark dire sanctions are applied.

Rumour has it that several players on both sides are about to be sent off. It's not that they've done anything wrong, you understand, but the refs are getting unpopular with the crowd and sending players off is a quick way of demonstrating their power, and more important, that the game simply couldn't proceed safely and happily without all those refs in place. The refs have the trump card, you see. They've managed to fool the crowd into believing that they are there to ensure good football is played. The crowd don't understand enough to realise that good football and compliance with the rule book are vastly different things.

So now the players are all back in their places. The crowd is unhappy but silent. After all, they know these players wouldn't be there if it wasn't for the refs, and without the refs play would be dirty, wouldn't it? So the game is about to start. Again.

Three refs...

All about to blow their whistles in unison when...

One of them suggests to the other two that given all the new regulations, the players probably won't be able to do a proper job without lots of training. That would be training in the new rules, you understand, not in football. These players are marvellous footballers. Some of them are international and historical icons. But the new rules? Well the rules are a completely different matter. Although... hmmm... on the other hand maybe the refs should require the players to *prove* they're good footballers after all, even if they've been playing all their lives and by their ability alone have reached the FA Cup Final. You just can't be too sure, can you? And, well, if the refs think that's the right thing to do, well they must know best. Cos after all they're the refs. That's what we pay them for. Isn't it? Isn't it?

So the refs decide to send the players away on a training course. Well, lots of training courses, actually; for the rest of the season, actually.

Not to worry about the cost. The match fees can be increased – lots of the spectators can afford to pay far more, can't they? And lots of players are paid far too much, aren't they? There's plenty of fat to be trimmed in this game, oh yes indeed. So we'll just cut what we pay them. We'll tell the crowd that the match is postponed until:

- The players are better trained
- The ethnic mix of the teams is sounder and gender unbiased
- The teams have undertaken crowd surveys that prove they're playing the kind of game the crowd wants to watch
- The seats in the stands have been refurbished at the expense of the teams, each one having the refs' logo imprinted on it
- The popcorn stands are offering allergen free, nut free, fat free, vegan compatible, humanely slaughtered, individually wrapped, date stamped, ingredient specified, individualised, personalised, pasteurised, analysed, verified homogenised, sterilised, popcorn kernels.

The crowd go home mumbling, wondering why it's necessary to have all this regulation now when ten years ago none of it was necessary.

No one plays football anymore

You can't get anyone to sign on as a team captain – the likelihood of criminal prosecution is overwhelming, and who wants to work with that kind of threat hanging over them?

Players don't want to play in case they're suspended pending investigation that they kicked the ball with the wrong foot (suspension is, they are told, a neutral act. But it doesn't feel so neutral when you're sitting at home staring at the walls, wondering what on earth you've done to deserve it).

And because no one plays any more no one needs refs any more.

But please don't worry about the refs. They now spend all their time going to refs' conferences on how to get the game going again. And that will of course require far more regulation.

Except for those refs who have retired on huge pensions. Well, something had to be done with all that money the payers had accumulated, didn't it?

And really, you know, the world's a much better place without football.

Isn't it?

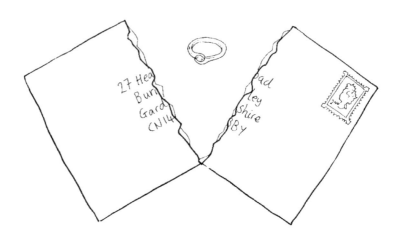

21 You Say Goodbye

Dear Hilary

I have no intention of sending you this letter. But I know you of all people would understand my need to write it anyway. A friend of mine says that writing is free therapy for the soul. But I find myself wanting to challenge each of those words – free, therapy and soul. The cost of writing this may not be measured in the passing of coin, but it is there in the flow of tears. Therapy? I don't think so. Therapy, as you constantly tell me, is supposed to effect lasting change but I wake to the same loss and pain and emptiness day after day. And soul? Now that you are gone I have none.

You told me some days ago that you would give me your final answer by today, and this morning you came to deliver it. When you arrived I could see before you told me that you had been crying, and from that I knew what your decision was.

The problem we have each had in the declining weeks of our marriage is actually coming to any decision at all, for we are both torn beyond our capacity for rational thought. There has been so much good that has passed between us in twenty years that it is hard beyond comprehension to contemplate ending our life together, even though it is now over four months since you moved out. I ask myself how it can be that simultaneously I worship the ground on which you walk and explode with frustration at your seeming inability to contemplate the pain you cause me. I know you feel the same. There is cancer in this relationship. Its body is at war with itself and is losing the battle against the creeping decay.

I do not blame you for what is happening now. I don't think I even blame myself at this moment. Though in the times of pain that will surely come when my demons are unleashed, I know I will alternate between rage that you have brought us to this and

149

remorseful sorrow that my insufficiency to meet your changing needs has caused you to do so.

You were in the kitchen with Seb when I came in. There was a moment of eerie normality filled with superficial talk. I guess none of us knew quite what to say to one another. Seb's the best thing that ever happened to this marriage, to me, to you. We used to agonize over how our child would handle the difference between himself and his friends who had parents of different sexes. We used to worry that when puberty came he would turn out to be straight. Then we worried that he would be gay. Maybe we just needed to worry. Parents do that. And now Seb has gotten so far over her sexuality she doesn't give a shit about it, or ours for that matter.

Being all too aware of what needed to be said, I asked Seb to leave as gently as I could. Then I sat across the corner of the table from you as I have done for more years than I can begin to call to mind. The dishwasher and the washing machine chugged away, an unremitting movie score of domestic inconsequence against which we would play the final exit scene of our life together.

You mumbled a few preliminaries of no consequence, as if doing so would postpone the announcement of the decision just a little longer. So to make it easier I asked if you had arrived at that decision.

You said you couldn't come back to live with me... *at the moment.* Then you devastated me by saying you were afraid of returning. I asked you if you seriously thought I could contemplate doing you physical harm. Hilary, in all of our life together I have never laid a violent hand upon you. Yet you feared the violence of my words of this last year and the possibility that I might repeat them. Neither of us has ever needed physical brutality in order to wound. Words of violence have always lacerated sufficiently.

How cold it seems now to be recording this exchange in black and white. How little ability I have to convey the colour of the emotion we were both feeling only two hours ago, into the monochrome of a Word document. I've changed my mind. I will send this letter to you. You deserve to know how I am feeling right at this moment. You need to be made aware of the gut-stabbing, soul-ripping flesh-burning pain for which you are responsible.

I know now beyond doubting that what you say is true. I could have coped more easily if you were leaving me for another man. But to tell me that your wish was now to find a woman to live with was more than I wanted to absorb. And hardest of all is your constant insistence that there is no other specific person you are leaving me for; it is simply that you can no longer pretend to be gay. Pretend? Is that all you've done these last twenty years?. I know you too well for that. I've known every centimetre of your body and soul. So don't give me pretend. I know damn well what was real and what wasn't.

Then there was a silence while we simply sat there, looking at each other sorrowfully. Then came the tears. From both of us. And at that moment I wanted nothing more than to take you to bed. But I knew that you would not come. So we stood there in the kitchen, and instead I hugged you for what must be the last time. You said there would be more hugs. I listened to the coffee dripping through the filter behind me and knew you were wrong. There can be no more holding onto you. I have to learn to let you go.

For want of something practical to do, I went out to clean up the deck while you looked for Seb to tell her your decision. My hands sank into practicality and my mind busied itself with the formation of these words that I knew I would need to write. It's such a strange way to end a relationship. But emotion runs at light speed and I need to slow my world down to a pace my consciousness can manage. Such is the need of the meaning-making creature. Thus do I celebrate my fragile humanity.

Maybe thirty minutes later I looked up and saw you standing, watching me from twenty feet away. I smiled and felt the passion arc between us once more. It will continue to do so from time to time. It's too much to expect it to stop instantly. Suppressing my love for you is going to take a long, long time. And somewhere in my heart it will always remain, locked quietly away, however much I try to pretend it has gone. I put down the broom and came over to you. I took your hands and looked into your eyes. I told you that if this was really happening, if we were not simply acting out soap opera scenes, I needed, properly and finally, to say goodbye to you. So we stood there looking at each other. I took you in my arms and kissed you a final time. I hope I will remember the feel of your lips on mine forever. I hope the memory of your body pressed against mine will never end. Right now, I hope that when my personal ending finally comes, these will be my last memories in my last moments of life, as my consciousness finally slips away.

But that old devil, rational thought, tells me it will not be so. We will go our separate ways and make a future without each other, regardless of how hard I find it to contemplate doing so at present. Each of us will grieve for the death of our life together with whatever rituals the culture of our separating souls requires. Then, impossible as it seems right now, it will be over and we will both move on to become people we have yet to meet. How strange is our mortality, made as it is of these commencements and completions.

Whatever my future may hold, Hilary, I needed that final moment with you. I released you from that last marital embrace, and watched you turn and walk away. I followed a little way, so that I could watch you turn the car around and leave.

I stood and watched as your BMW disappeared down the drive. Your left indicator came on for no one in particular to see, then you were gone.

I looked up into an ice blue sky, and contemplated my singular unimportance to a continuing universe.

22   Samphire

When they said we smelled of samphire and ocean salt their intent was kindness. In truth the odour that clung to us was nothing more than that of obnoxious bodily fluids and the twisted dreams of old men hobbling towards the grave.

We had, all three of us, arrived at the shelter within hours of each other on 19th December 2014. Though we shared nothing more than a moment, to those that looked on it was sufficient synchronicity at that pre-festive moment, to christen us 'The Three Kings'. Once this seasonal nomination had been universally adopted my two unintended associates were henceforth known as Gold and Frankincense and I as Myrrh. There could be no more fitting a name for me.

Though our cotemporaneous arrival was nothing more than coincidence, the fact that it took place on 19th December was not. We had each in our time stayed at St Solomon's Shelter for the Homeless before. Each of us knew that its policy of moving residents on within three days was relaxed during the week before and the week after Christmas. And though it was profoundly disagreeable to be ejected from our beds on New Year's Day to face a city like as not frozen to several degrees below zero, we all considered this a small price to pay for the luxury of two weeks punctuated by hot showers, and characterised by prolific warmth and sufficiency of food.

We were to receive an improbable visit from Santa Claus that year. It was due entirely to the strict 'no alcohol' policy maintained by St Solomon's. Signs as to the inviolable nature of this rule and the terminal consequences of its breech were posted at frequent intervals around the hostel. They were also explained to each man upon admittance. Why anyone would squander thoughtlessly the benefits we valued so highly on momentary stupefaction escapes my reason, for detection was inevitable and ejection from the shelter just as certain. But there again I am not an alcoholic. As it was, at 10.00 am on December 23rd, Frankincense grudgingly vacated the bed next to mine, packed his bag and left, a volley of incoherent but nevertheless incendiary expletives trailing out behind him until the closing of the door severed it. His bed remained vacant for a little under half an hour according to the plastic clock on the pine boarded wall of the dormitory.

The man shown to the vacant bed by the staff worker was a similar age to most of us who entered the shelter, that is, wholly indeterminate. He could have been anywhere between twenty-five and seventy-five. His skin behind the grime was olive coloured as far as I could tell, suggesting a Mediterranean origin. His beard was a greyish white, at least a month old, his hair unkempt and his face ingrained with the encrusted dirt of too many days on the road. In other words, he looked much as all of us did upon admission. What distinguished him was not his initial appearance but his voice. For there emanated from his barely parted lips an incessant stream of mumbles in a language clearly foreign, but which I could not easily identify. As it happens, I am fluent in German and Spanish, and speak passable Pashto and a little Dari. Something in his speech was familiar in the context of those latter languages, but if it was Arabic I could not yet pinpoint which dialect. His posture was bent and his gait shuffling. Somewhere along his journey he had encountered some seasonally mirthful individual who had provided him with clothing in the form of a Santa Claus suit, now, of course, dirty, torn and stained. Nevertheless it was all he possessed and he continued to cling to it despite the protestations of the shelter workers. Presumably he did not understand its cultural significance. Finally a compromise was reached despite the language barrier, whereby it was understood and agreed that while he bathed, his garments would be washed and dried, then returned to him. To no one's surprise he was immediately christened Santa.

A little before noon Santa re-emerged from the shower room, not exactly fragrant – that would typically take two or three more extended periods under the hot shower. However, he had at least shed the odour that the shelter workers euphemistically referred to as samphire. He returned to his bed and sat down, eying

156

suspiciously all those of us who chose to be in the dormitory at that moment. From his arrival onwards Santa displayed the erratic behaviour of the deeply disturbed.

Inevitably most of those who sojourn at the St Solomon's shelter or others like it, are the walking wounded of a dissociated society that would mostly prefer to behave as if they did not exist. If you want to be generous at Christmas most people find it easier to send a donation to the Daily Telegraph annual appeal, or better still to Battersea Dogs home. Such gifts afford the donor the opportunity of a cosy feeling of generosity, a reassuring confidence that however much they spend on themselves or the over-privileged circle of well-stuffed family and friends around them, they did not fail to remember the 'less fortunate' at Christmas. The newspaper cutting, or the iPhoned credit card number, or the appealing picture of a cute puppy retorts nothing in response that might disturb the warm glow of self-satisfaction that is, for most of you, an essential part of the festive season. But God forbid that you should ever make it through the doors of St. Solomon's or any of a hundred shelters like it up and down the land either as a helper or, like me, the personified excrement of a myopic self-absorbed uber-class. If you did, the reality of what 'life' means to the majority of the world's population would sink a dagger between your eyes and insert into the open wound enough metaphoric salt as to have you rubbing the incision for the rest of your life. You think I go too far in disturbing your self-satisfied indolence? Then let me tell you about Christmas in Helmand outside the military cordon, Christmas on the streets Bagdad or —.

But then again, this is not my story I'm telling you, it's Santa's. Mine can wait a little while yet.

So he returned from his shower, and sat naked on his bed until the Santa suit was returned to him, clean, if no less torn than it had been when it was taken from him. He remained there in Buddha-like entranced immobility when it was offered back to him, gazing up into the eyes of the young centre worker who was holding it out with, I would guess, genuine warmth in his smile.

"Thank you," Santa finally said in the first words of English I had heard him speak. They were heavily accented words, words that carried an air of surprise if not suspicion, almost as if he were implying there had to be a catch to such an act of selfless generosity. But the young man continued to smile his honest smile and gestured that Santa should take the clothes. Finally he opened his arms literally if not metaphorically and took the ragged suit back, whereupon he continued to sit unmoving, the garments draped across his lap as the come-and-go bustle of the dormitory continued around him. At suppertime we all moved into the dining room, leaving Santa behind us, still unmoving. When I finished supper I wanted to bring with me a plate of pasta for Santa. Such transport of food beyond doorway of the dining room contravened the rules of the hostel. I was not about to see myself follow Frankincense into the frozen world outside, so I explained the situation to a senior hostel worker who approved my intended act. Accordingly I carried back to the dormitory a plate of spaghetti in tomato sauce and a spoon, a fork and a knife, figuring he would prefer to cut it up rather than try to wind it into consumable sized pieces. But when I got back to my bed he was asleep, his red trousers on in normal fashion and his oversize jacket covering his shoulders like a blanket. I left the food and the cutlery on the bedside cabinet for when he awoke and joined the others in the lounge for the evening's TV. On my return just before lights out he was still sleeping, though fitfully, and his vellicated movements had tossed his red jacket onto the floor, leaving his torso naked to the cold of the night. He was sleeping face down. I readied myself for bed and for sleep.

I cannot say what time I woke – I do not own a watch. The one I possessed in my former life was stolen from me during my first week on the streets and I knew if I acquired a replacement it too would disappear in similar fashion. I learned quickly that chronology has little significance to me and those like me. We are they who exist outside of time, whose 'before' and 'after,' whose 'yesterday' and 'tomorrow' are so similar to our 'now' as to confer an irrelevance upon time itself. You and those like you dream of inventing a machine to take you into the past or future. We are they who live our future today and will live our past tomorrow. You dream of inventing an elixir of youth, or an anti-aging cream that will preserve your life eternally. We have already discovered the true secret of everlasting life for the monotonous ache of eternity echoes incessantly through the empty caverns of our souls.

What woke me, though, was the fact that Santa's fitful, agitated sleep was now punctuated with a delirium of speech that, so far as I could tell, crossed the boundaries of language as easily as asylum seekers cross the boarders of continental Europe in pursuit of the Shangri-La beyond La Manche.

I propped myself up in bed on my left elbow facing him. Through the darkness I could see, but much more clearly hear, his torment. I reached out my hand, intending to rouse him from his terror filled nightmares, but hesitated momentarily. And as I did, he sat bolt upright in bed, his face contorted and his eyes wide open in the manner of men who have long since abandoned sanity. In his continuing sleep he grabbed me by the shoulders with a grip so tight I could not free myself. For a moment he seemed to struggle to find words, then said to me in a loud whisper in English,

"My sleigh... knife... faster than bullet... I cannot forget... never forget... presents of the childrens. My sleigh... childrens. Presents of childrens... always with me." Then with no warning and without turning his face from me, his right hand released my left shoulder and reached to the bedside cabinet where his meal had long since gone cold. He picked up the knife and drew it slowly across his chest from his left shoulder to beneath his right breast. I recoiled rapidly, instinctively fearful that he would turn the knife on me in his frenzy. But he released it and it clattered onto the boarded floor as the shallow, fifty centimetre gash across his torso turned slowly red and oozed blood onto his legs where it seeped silently and invisibly into the red material. "My sleigh. Presents of childrens," he said calmly, "I never stop presents of childrens. Forgive. Padre. Forgive. God."

I took a decision at that point – an event so infrequent to one in my position as to be describable almost as a luxury. I could have roused the dormitory and called the duty officer. But if I had, Santa would have been ejected from the shelter at first light. Instead I lead him to the toilets at the end of the dormitory and staunched his bleeding with toilet paper while he watched me silently, his mournful eyes conveying everything he wished to communicate. The incision looked far worse than it was and clearly he, like me, had experienced worse wounds in too terrible a past to confront. Nevertheless, that past was seeping through the

159

cracks of time and into the present once again in a manner all too familiar to us, the eternally damned.

Finally he allowed me to lead him back to bed where I settled him under his red jacket, for he still would not lie under the blankets and sheets. Amazingly all this had been accomplished without waking anyone else. As his breathing settled I returned to my own bed. As I lay in the darkness, too animated to sleep, I was at last able to turn my thoughts to his words and I reviewed what I knew:

An olive skinned man dressed in a Santa suit arrives at an English hostel for the homeless just before Christmas. Speaking of sleighs and children's presents he appears to believe he is Santa Claus. And most uncanny in all of this he addresses me as Padre and asks for forgiveness of sins. It is over five years since I was last addressed as Padre.

I fell asleep turning these words over and over in my mind confused as to what manner of delirium could cause a man to believe he was Santa Claus. But in truth I was far more concerned about being addressed as Padre. For this was a term that belonged in the past I wanted to forget and it seemed that for me too, the past was seeping into the present and threatened to determine the future.

I awoke to the general bustle of a communal sleeping area rousing. Men moved about me, up and down the narrow corridor between our beds to the showers and WCs. Men retrieved shirts from hangers hooked over window latches to dry in contravention of the shelter's minor rules. Men retrieved toothpaste and brushes from secret compartments in their rucksacks. The values conferred on minor objects by those who possess almost nothing will seem strange to those who own everything they could want and more than they will ever need.

I turned to Santa's bed, but he was gone. Since he had left his red tunic I presumed he was showering and intended to return. When he did, the cut across his chest look sore but shallow. It was not bleeding. Santa smiled at me, though did not speak. Even to be acknowledged was, I thought, progress.

At 8.00 am by the dormitory clock we were ushered out and into the dining room. This time Santa came too, shuffling forward in the line like a natural. I went first and he took his lead from me. After breakfast we were free to do as we pleased. However, few chose to go out into the near freezing temperatures of a Christmas Eve morning. I sat in the lounge reading a two-year-old magazine while the television grumbled in the corner. Santa seemed content to sit by me silently. After lunch those that wished to sleep were permitted back into the dormitory. I exercised the option, as did two or three others not wishing to pass the opportunity of a soft bed, regardless of the time of day. Santa followed. As I lay down onto my bed he imitated me and was soon asleep. Then so was I.

I was woken by a violent shaking. I opened my eyes, still disorientated, to find Santa gripping my arm as the fire alarm went off. He was wide eyed and wild eyed with terror and yelled at me, "Padre! Padre! Incoming. Incoming," as he tried to drag me from where I lay and down into the narrow space between my bed and his.

As I shook sleep from my head I said, "No Santa. No incoming. It's the fire alarm test."

Then it was "Padre! Padre! Fire! Fire!"

Clearly I was to be granted no further sleep that Christmas Eve afternoon and for want of something better to do, decided to take Santa out for a walk. He seemed to understand readily and acquiesced with no resistance. As we left the hostel the festivities were in full swing about us with carols emanating from the shop doorways, chuggers' collection tins being rattled in everyone's faces, and later shoppers heaving parcels home barely in time for Christmas Day. At first Santa seemed to enjoy the level of activity we had stepped into and he eyed the activity as if he had never seen it before. This of course could not have been the case since he had come to the hostel only a little over twenty-four hours earlier and must have passed through similar waves of humanity to reach St Solomon's.

Inevitably we had not ventured far before fingers started pointing at his red suit. Santa did not seem to mind this at first. It was only when the children began to notice and crowd towards him his eyes filled with tears and he fell to his knees sobbing and rocking backwards and forwards. "Padre," he managed between sobs, "Padre. My sleigh... the childrens. Presents of the childrens. Always I have presents of the childrens." Then he turned his face

161

to heaven and wailed so pitifully that all the little ones assembled backed away to their parents, uncertain as to how to respond to the unlikely sight of Santa Claus on his knees, weeping.

We were becoming a focal point and it would not be long before some voice of authority arrived to threaten us with action for disturbing the peace. I ushered Santa gently to his feet and led him, still weeping, back to the hostel. There I sat him on his bed, eased him gently back to the supine and waited until he drifted into an exhausted sleep. At bed time he was still sleeping.

Predictably, I was woken in the night. Again I am unable to say at what time for certain, but I did not feel I had slept for long. This time, as he shook me from sleep it became quickly evident that this was no nightmare on his part. He was fully awake and seemingly, perhaps for the first time since we had met, in his right mind.

As he continued to shake my arm, he spoke to me rationally. It was a few moments before I realised he was speaking in Pashto.

كنت أتكلم الباشتو بادري ؟

"You speak Pashto, Padre? How is it you speak Pashto?" I can only assume that it had been my turn to talk in my sleep and it was this that had woken him. Was this the first time he had heard a familiar language so far from home? As I gradually came fully into the waking state, the conversation continued in Pashto, on his side fluently and on mine in a halting approximation. And on we talked, on through the night, through the barriers of language and culture, through the walls of fear and anger that we build to hide our self-loathing from one another.

I have thought back to that night many times, wondering what turn of coincidence or synchronicity had brought us together as Christmas day dawned over a sleeping city. Did we seek catharsis? Did we somehow permit ourselves the insouciant hope that the makeshift confessional we shared in the dark dormitory that night would somehow open the gates of the Celestial City on Christmas Day? For as it was, gates did open, but behind them lay not the gardens and fountains of joy with which we might once have populated our dreams of the future, but our own personal Belsens where the emaciated victims of our past crimes lay, stacked higher into the sky than a man's vision can penetrate.

His story and mine were not so dissimilar despite our backgrounds. I can blame no one but myself that following university I chose first to enter upon Catholic ordination and then, following the minimum ministerial experience period, the British army chaplaincy. I will not bore you with my years of field service prior to Helmand. Suffice to say that it was routine to the point of monotony. And it could easily have continued that way were it not for my confessional experiences of 2008–2009. When a man comes to you and confesses participation in the killing of innocents, do you grant him absolution? If his heart is repentant and the event unintended, you do, surely. When a second man enters behind the curtain and speaks of his torn conscience as one who has witnessed deliberate killings of civilians, how do you advise him? And when another and another and another follow them, speaking of the murder of non-combatants, do you condemn or do you absolve? Do you advise confidential conversations with commanding officers when you know their likely complicity in these acts? Do you recommend that distraught men who have participated in such acts by-pass the chain of command, knowing that the army will quite literally close ranks against such threats? Or do you, as I did, run out of platitudes with which to reassure others and yourself and eventually have nowhere to turn, not to God and not to man, and thus do the running out yourself. For that was what happened to me in Helmand. I ran out of resources, ran out of faith and ran out of the British Army.

And thus it was I found myself in another quasi-confessional that night, or at least in the presence of a man who needed desperately to confess his sins. Yet however anguish-laden my personal history, I could not have conceived of the unutterable pain suffered by the man before me, a fellow priest it transpired, in his case from the Nestorian Church in which he had cared for the souls of several Christian villages outside Mosul.

"Daesh came… June 2014," he started uncertainly. "The peoples… they had run from them from other villages. They told us Daesh kill. Daesh… rapio?"

"Rape," I corrected.

"Yes, rape. And kill like this." He drew his palm across his throat.

"Beheading," I ventured despite my distaste at the term.

"Yes, Daesh behead. Daesh rapio. Daesh kill. The men. The women. The childrens."

"Rape and behead children," I queried, "is that really what you mean?"

"Yes. Is so."

Thus, while the world looked on in astounded disbelief that such cruelties could be perpetrated in the name of a loving Allah, the army of darkness swept through village after village, destroying, pillaging, raping, murdering. Such was the way that news travels, the village in which Santa was teaching school in the church that day had but hours' notice of the approaching army and its nefarious deeds. Many parents came quickly, took their precious children and fled.

"Parents come," he continued. "Take childrens. Run. Daesh reach village. Still I have childrens, Padre. Six childrens. Small." At this point he gestured with his palm to indicate children of perhaps eight years of age or less. "Two boy. Four girl."

"I know Daesh is comings. Rapio childrens. Beheads. Burn bodies. Make watch."

He looked at me, huge sad tears rolling down his face, not knowing whether I would scream condemnation at him or take him in my arms.

"So I take childrens. One on one."

"One by one?" I ventured.

"Yes, one by one. Back of church. Behind…"

He was lost for the word in English.

"Behind the alter?' I questioned, my voice sticking in my throat.

He nodded. Then his words ceased and he gestured, representing his drawing a knife across each small throat, his right hand high above his left shoulder sweeping down across the child he held close to his heart for their last living moments upon the earth, just as he had done in his sleep the night before.

"I lay childrens here," he said, miming his laying each child before the cross of his Saviour and then waiting for the army of Satan. And as he waited in the darkness he felt, as he told me that Christmas morning, neither shame nor sorrow nor fear. All there was, was the church and the children and the alter and the

164

blood. And he waited. And he waited. And he waited, for an end that never came.

"ISIS… not come to church. Like angel of death pass over Israel in Egypt. I wait. Wait. Wait. Wait. No ISIS. When I understand this I leave church. I leave childrens in church. I look for parents. No find." His words came erratically through his tears. He wiped his hands perpetually over his face as if he could wipe away those tears and his words and his past in a single action.

During the following six months, if he is to be believed, Santa walked openly out of Syria and across Turkey, passing through Greece and Italy, boarding ferries and crossing frontiers without money and without being challenged. And all along his way he took food from shops and street vendors without being seen as if he were invisible to all, as if he had the mark of Cain upon him. Finally on that cold December morning he had arrived at St Solomon's in a Santa Claus suit with six months' encrusted dirt sticking to his body and a hardened layer of indifference clinging to his soul. And here, due to the ambiguities of the English language and his ignorance of English grammar, he spoke in his sleep of what I, his hearer, took as 'My Sleigh… childrens,' when a more fluent speaker might have said 'I slayed children.' And when I understood him to say the 'presents of the childrens' were always with him, what he was seeking to convey was that 'the presence of the children was always with him,' for never, never could he forget the unforgivable sin he had perpetrated in the name of preventing an even grosser evil.

And so it was that before that dawn on Christmas morning, he asked me,

"Padre, you forgive sin, please?" even though he knew I could not.

My inevitable answer, "Only God forgives sin, Santa," was met with the response,

"Then you kill with knife. If you will not forgive Padre, please, you must kill." All this was said after the tears had ceased flowing. Now his face betrayed no more emotion than the stains of his earlier weeping. His own life meant nothing to him. All that remained for him was a hope that somehow the pain might be brought to an end.

Both I and the world had come full circle that Christmas morning. The world confronted yet again the slaughter of the innocents that purportedly had accompanied that first Christmas tide. And I personally faced yet again the request that I absolve the unabsolvable.

I did not grant him absolution. I did not kill him.

I never knew his name.

23   The Secret of the Perfect Vegetarian Risotto for One

The secret of the Perfect Vegetarian Risotto for Two lies in combining precisely the right ingredients, cooked in precisely the correct order, for precisely the optimum cooking time. It helps enormously if you have had precisely twenty-six years' experience in doing so.

You must first set aside:
- one carrot
- one onion
- two small courgettes
- six medium sized mushrooms
- four cloves of garlic (crushed)
- salt and pepper
- one green pepper
- eight ounces of Arborio rice
- one and a half pints of stock made from two Oxo vegetable stock cubes and a bottle of white Italian wine 'Pinot Grigio', which you will have first discovered on honeymoon in Tuscany twenty-six years ago to the day.

Use of any other ingredients in any other proportions will be detrimental to the result overall.

The wine should be topped up to the one and a half pint mark with Malvern Still Spring Water. This is in commemoration of the many weekends you will have spent driving the roads of the Malvern Hills for no better reason than to drop your husband off at the commencement of his hike and later pick him up at a precise time of his specification at another specified location. Arriving late at the specified location will be detrimental to the marriage overall.

The Pinot Grigio/water mix should be placed in the microwave for exactly four and a half minutes on a high setting before the addition of the Oxo cubes. Heating for any longer will be detrimental to the result overall.

The Perfect Vegetarian Risotto for Two is always, always, always made on a Friday evening and must be ready at precisely 7.00 pm when your husband will walk through the door from 'the gym', which he has visited on his way home from work almost unfailingly for the last twenty-six years. Serving the Perfect Vegetarian Risotto for Two late will be very, very detrimental to the marriage overall.

You are advised to lay the dining table by 6.07 pm, placing the table mats, cutlery, glasses, condiments and wine cooler in precisely the same locations each week (a soft tape measure is helpful for this purpose; metal tape measures should be avoided, due to their propensity to scratch tables when held in severely shaking hands). Failure to place the items precisely is unlikely to be detrimental to the result overall. However, it will contribute to the diminution of the emotional wellbeing of the cook.

Commence preparation of the food at 6.11 pm by slicing the vegetables into similarly sized pieces. Should the size of the pieces vary significantly, cut the larger ones again until they are all similarly sized. Failure to do so will result in some of the pieces being over cooked and others undercooked. This will be detrimental to the result overall. It may also have the unanticipated consequence of causing your husband to lock you out of the house overnight. Should this occur in mid-January, when it is snowing, and should you live in the Lake District National Park, some 1.37 miles from the nearest neighbour, this will be detrimental to your health overall.

Next, at 6.27 pm and 30 seconds, add the salt, pepper and crushed garlic to the Arborio rice and begin frying the mixture in an appropriate quantity of Tuscan extra virgin olive oil. It is essential that the oil must, without fail, be Tuscan. This is so even if you do not know how to recognise Tuscan extra virgin olive oil, even if there are no shops locally that sell Tuscan extra virgin olive oil, even if Tuscan extra virgin olive oil tastes precisely the same as all other extra virgin olive oils and even if you have no money with which to buy Tuscan extra virgin olive oil. While failure to use Tuscan extra virgin olive oil will not be detrimental to the result overall, it can result in bottle breakages and the application of broken glass to your forearms and wrists.

Leaving the oil bottle on the kitchen worktop after you have used it can have either positive or negative results, depending on the mood of your husband when he comes through the door. Sometimes it has been known to lead to husbands reminiscing positively about their honeymoons. On such occasions you must expect that after dinner sexual activity of a variety specified by your husband will be required. Failure to acquiesce to his choice of sexual activity, however unpalatable, will be detrimental to the marriage overall and may result in severe bruising and tearing of sensitive tissue. Alternatively, if your husband's disposition on coming through the door is negative, sight of the Tuscan extra virgin olive oil bottle may result in aggressive language connected with his regret at "being conned into marrying you all those years ago, you fucking bitch." Bruising, broken limbs and tearing of sensitive tissue has not been known on such occasions, but cannot be ruled out. On balance, leaving the oil bottle on the kitchen worktop is not recommended.

At 6.31 pm and 15 seconds, begin adding the stock slowly to the rice and stir continuously. At 6.32 pm precisely begin the addition of the carrots. Should this be your twenty-sixth wedding anniversary, you are advised to avoid thinking about your husband's failure ever to remember to give you an anniversary card, a cheap bunch of flowers from the petrol station or even so much as a bar of fucking chocolate. Experience has shown this to result in heightened emotions which can cause the cook to forget the precise cooking times that are required in the making of the Perfect Vegetarian Risotto for Two. It can also result in uncontrollable tears which can drip from the cook's face into the cooking liquid which will be detrimental to the result overall.

At 6.38 pm add more stock and the onions. Continue stirring.

At 6.45 pm add more stock and the courgettes. Continue stirring

At 6.51 pm add the remaining stock and the mushrooms. Continue stirring until all the liquid is absorbed. Leaving any liquid in the bottom of the pan risks its later use in deliberate scalding which will be detrimental to your health overall.

At 6.54 pm serve the Perfect Vegetarian Risotto for Two onto two heated plates and place into the oven to keep warm.

Between 6.55 pm and 6.59 pm, clear the kitchen, while recalling through your tears the text your husband had omitted to remove from the screen of his phone the previous evening before falling into a drunken stupor. Even if you are sobbing uncontrollably and cannot recall the exact words, it is important to remember that they read something like "Hey babes, I'm sooooo horny for you. My legs are open and my pussy's wet. See you tomorrow at 4.00 in the usual place."

At 7.00 pm precisely, when your husband walks through the kitchen door, after twenty-six years of acquiescence to his every whim, loose control.

Grab the carving knife you left unconsciously on the kitchen work top by the door and, using an upward curved motion, stab it repeatedly into the left side of his chest, screaming "Bastard, bastard, bastard," through your tears in time with each stab. Tears will not be detrimental to the result overall. Novice wielders of knives may be unsure as to how many applications of the knife are required to terminate the heart's activity. However, the Coroner will later report that twenty-six were more than sufficient to stop it from beating.

When you are certain your husband is dead, wipe your tears and call the police. Given the support of a good barrister and sympathetic jury, it will not be long before you are able to settle down to the Perfect Vegetarian Risotto for One. Your husband's absence from your life will not be detrimental to your future overall.

24   The Nazis in the Blanket Chest

It never was a bed, you understand. It was a Cromwell tank, full of cannon and machine guns, smelling of diesel from the fuel tank and cordite from the ammunition pile. From the security of our armoured vehicle we would pound the German positions mercilessly for a full thirty minutes after lights out. Some might have smelled starch as they slithered like fishes down between crisp, freshly laundered linen sheets. But we were hardened soldiers at the battlefront. All we knew were the deprivations of war and such rations as we could secret from the kitchen before being hounded to our tank by the generals and senior officers. How unfair that they would sit up late downstairs, reading dispatches from HQ and listening to the wireless for coded signals that would disclose enemy positions, while we were obliged to protect them on the front line of the darkness upstairs.

Periodically we would launch a daring assault behind the enemy lines of the open bedroom window. There we would happen upon the vicious Hun, cunningly disguised as next-door's cat. Without hesitation, we would take prisoner this servant of evil and question it under merciless water torture. Always, though, when its howls of protest became excessive, there would be negotiations between the senior officers of each side, and inevitably we would be forced to relinquish our prisoner, wet and miserable but otherwise unharmed, to the safety of its home territory.

By daylight you would have seen a blanket chest in the corner of that room. But we knew that under cover of darkness the camouflage would be thrown back and the concrete bunker concealed underneath would spit venom and steel towards us as we protected ourselves with armour plate that by day had been disguised as old cardboard boxes. Outside, the flickering of sodium streetlights would announce the commencement of hostilities, as they transformed themselves into searchlights sweeping across the night sky, seeking for the first signs of Stuka dive bombers and Focke-Wulf fighters. We could hear the aircraft droning away over the road that marked our version of the white cliffs of Dover. Never did we see one of these elusive craft, however. They evidently preferred to remain tarmac-bound safe from the dog fights we were certain we could hear hundreds of feet above us.

There were flags and insignia a-plenty back then, too. Union jacks of coloured crayon would wave proudly over our encampment, confronting enemy swastikas formed in the daylight hours from bent twigs brought in from the forest. And if, in the light of the following morning, our detritus was cleared away by the merciless dustpans and vacuum cleaners of reconstruction, well, there would always be time to fashion replacement emblems before the next night's hostilities commenced.

Being older, Stephen was better than me at inventing the histories that lent realism to our various conflicts. He was better, too at conjuring ever more lurid forms of injury that he claimed to have befallen him through the bravery of his fighting, or those that happened to me merely because I was a less experienced soldier who failed to respond willingly to his commands. Sometimes, if he were the injured one, he would need treatment in the field hospital of the bathroom where I, as medical orderly, would be required to minister to his heroic wounds with toilet paper and toothbrush. When it was me that was injured, I would be forced to endure my exile alone in the field hospital, while he held the front line single handed until he felt I had learned sufficiently the obligations of follower-ship to return to shadow of his heroism.

I bore my subservience stoically in all circumstances save one. When he feigned death, the rules of war required that I counted to fifty before he could be legitimately revived. But should I falter in this challenging task and forget which number came after twenty-seven, or skip all the thirties through boredom, he would resolutely refuse to rise from the dead. Then I would weep real tears, lest this time he truly be gone and I would be left to face the Nazis alone. "It's fifty, Stevee," I would say. "I said fifty! Open your eyes, Stevee," I would shake him by the shoulder, urgently willing him to shrug off the dark shrouds of death. "I said fifty, Stevee. You have to be not dead now, Stevee. I said fifty! It's not fair!" Only when he considered I had suffered enough, or when he thought I was on the verge of summoning a General from downstairs to arbitrate the fairness or otherwise of death, would he be miraculously restored to perfect health like the immortal that all younger brothers secretly believe their elders to be.

Eventually, each nightly skirmish would end with one or other of us drifting off into a deep sleep, whereupon the enemy would cease fire in the most gentlemanly of fashions. They must, somehow, have been aware that a five-year-old and an eight-year-old need their sleep if they are to fight another night. So as the sounds of our regular breathing wafted across the battle lines to the enemy positions, the howitzers would morph back into curtain rails and the bunker would once more become a blanket chest.

After the funeral they gave me the flag from his coffin. I took the rest of the day off and drove down to our childhood home in Fordingbridge, only to discover that the old house had been knocked down to make way for flats. I wandered aimlessly for a while but nothing seemed familiar any more.

I spent the evening alone at home in front of an open fire with a bottle of Glenfiddich. As twilight fell, sodium streetlamps flickered into life reminding me of searchlights and dogfights. Glancing over at the old blanket chest in the inglenook, now in use as a log box, I wanted more than anything to see the lid being raised by the muzzle of a machine gun. When the whiskey had enough of a hold on me I went up to the bathroom and picked up my toothbrush and a half used toilet roll. I stared at them in my hands for a long, long time and wept real tears for the first time in forty years. "It's not fair, Stevee," I whispered under my breath, "You have to be not dead now." But try as I might, I couldn't remember how to count to fifty.

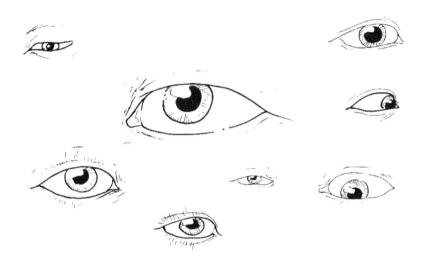

25   Counting Eyes

The walk from the turnstile to the far end of the pier is precisely 442 steps. You can check that if you want to, but I assure you it's correct. I count it every day – twice. There are many things I check. I always check whether I've turned the gas tap off before I go out. I turn it on and off 40 times just to be sure. Not 39 times, you understand, and not 41. I get to the bus stop to coincide with the arrival of the number 47 bus. I see no point in arriving more than 10 seconds early. Arriving 10 seconds late would severely disrupt my schedule. I can see from the way you're looking at me that you think a 10 second margin of error is still too much. I have to admit I lie awake at night considering that. I will modify my routines to reduce it to 8.5 seconds tomorrow and 7.75 the day after. Then we can review it – you and I together. That would be nice, wouldn't it? I have no one to review with now Andrea's gone and I'm sure you'd be just the person. You have the same eyes as Andrea – counting eyes.

I can't stop now. I'm on a tight schedule, you understand. Feel free to walk with me though. Take care not to step on the cracks between the boards or we'll have to go back to the beginning. I'm going to the end of the pier. It's 442 steps. You haven't forgotten that, have you? These things are hugely important, you know. Marcie was prone to forgetting the important things. Why, once I even had to enter her bathroom. I wasn't snooping, you understand, I had genuine suspicions. And anyway, she had left the window wide open. I found the plastic cap left off the fluoride toothpaste and the cold bath tap dripping. I know it's hard to believe, but it's true. I counted 102 drips. I screwed the toothpaste cap on and off 11 times so as to be certain it was properly sealed. I know you'll agree that I was right in issuing a stern reprimand.

When the shower is turned to the maximum temperature of 47 degrees it isn't dangerous. It just delivers a short, sharp shock and leaves a certain redness to the skin. Last calendar year we had an average of 0.41 ambulances per day pass up our street, and their sirens were sounding for an average of 72.49 seconds.

So here we are at the end of the pier. 442 steps. I was right, wasn't I? By the way, did I tell you I manage my food intake to maintain a precise balance with my expenditure of energy? So you'll understand that I can't share this cake with you. It contains 427 calories precisely. It would be very dangerous for me to share it with anyone else as I might not have the energy required to walk home. Denise didn't understand that. She tried to make a grab for the cake in this precise spot on a Sunday morning two years seven months and three days ago at 11.04 am. She was only being playful, of course. I knew that. And she knew I was only reacting playfully in return. She really should have learned to swim when I told her to.

I'm going from here to the café. You're welcome to join me for a regular sized cup of Ethiopian Arabica skinny latte if you wish, so long as you promise not to interrupt while I read *The Guardian* newspaper. If I'm interrupted I have to start again from the top left corner of the front page. You remember Janie, the barista in the café, don't you? She only interrupted me once – on Tuesday two weeks ago, at 11.46 am. I've counted 279 lampposts with her picture on so far. But it's a big job and I've not finished. We could complete the task together after I finish reading *The Guardian* newspaper. That will be at 12.22 pm assuming you don't interrupt me. You'd be really good at counting pictures on lampposts. You have counting eyes.

26   Drivers

Andrew is cycling into a waterfall. At least, he feels he is. The February rain is driving horizontally up the Banbury Road from the south. The 8.30 rush hour ignores the cycle lane and sweeps by, dragging a cold, wet wake that wraps around him from behind. He forces each foot down onto the pedals in turn, demanding the wheels to move, as if against their will, as if they are his slaves. His calf muscles have hardened to a texture that makes him think of iron each time he flexes them.

The rhythmic pressure of the pedals on his feet and the monotonous pin-pricks of the raindrops on his face induce a state of waking trance in which his thoughts drift to tonight; tonight, when his girl's fingers will stroke softly across those iron-textured muscles and Andrew will be distracted, his thoughts more ductile than metal. But such distractions are only temporary. When all is said and done, Clarissa is a necessity, even if a very enjoyable one at times. Andrew has, of course, considered the possibility of a future with her.

"Clarissa's a really lovely girl, Andy. Dad and I are so pleased you've found yourself someone special. I'd have thought that with her father a doctor and her from private school an' that, she'd be all airs and graces. But she loves Corrie just as much as I do, bless her. I don't think you'll find better. So if you was thinking, maybe... well, what I mean to say is, if you were minded to..."

But he is not. Clarissa is possessed of long, slim fingers that end in manicured nails, painted the colour of orgasm. Andrew greatly enjoys watching them when they are at work. Clarissa, has full lips, glossed with fire-red lipstick that matches her nails and a wide, wide smile that sometimes he is able to watch at work, and sometimes not. Clarissa is perfect – for now.

But as to the future, Andrew Chakra is dedicated to a Plan; indeed, so dedicated some call him fanatical. But actually, he rather likes that word. It speaks to him of single-mindedness, of passion, of a will to win – and of that oh-so-vital self-belief that he already knows lies at the root of all worthwhile achievement. Make no mistake about it. Andrew is already 'An Achiever', and nothing, but nothing will get in his way.

He covers the 2.3 miles to St Giles, looks repeatedly for a break in the traffic that will allow him to swing across for the right turn into Beaumont Street, but finds none. He dismounts and waltzes with the umbrella-covered nine-to-fivers. He watches them making their way from Gloucester Green to their desk chains, where they will serve their forty-seven year sentences until someone shakes them insincerely by the hand and presents them with a Taiwanese plastic carriage clock. Andrew has not got this far just to drive a desk and prize a worthless clock. He has already travelled a long way – East Finchley Comp via Haberdashers to a Classics Exhibition at Worcester is a lot further than the 75.2 miles indicated by map and slide rule.

"You've done it, lad. Your mother and I are proud of you. First person in the family to get into Oxford. Name on the honours board at Habs, Exhibition Scholarship at Worcester College – my boy's going to go far, no doubt about that!"

Andrew has every intention of going very far indeed – and of leaving the whole of his past behind him.

He arrives at the Lower Library, where his books and papers lay claim to the desk in the south west corner that overlooks the quad. So long as the librarian is not in the room, he will squander precious study time standing by the radiator to steam some of the rain out of his jeans and sweater. When they have dried a little he will turn to the day's work, a passage of Vedic Sanskrit for translation.

The sun is high now, but we force the slaves to work on. It burns their backs, covering their shoulders in great blisters. We aim our whips for these when they slacken their effort to concentrate their minds on their work. We do not permit the slaves to stop until it is too dark to see. Many have fallen where they laboured. We drag the dying away, leaving them for carrion on the mountain side and whip replacements into place from the cages. I watch them dig their heels into the loose stones as they struggle to get a grip. They put their shoulders against the platform and wait for the sound of the ram's horn – the command to push. As it wails down from the top of the mountain they heave forward as others pull on ropes from above. The ropes fail often. The slaves fail even more often.

Arran, Lord of Seers, has received a vision from Ra. In accordance with the vision we have placed the obelisk upon a wooden platform – and here is the brilliance of the vision. Under the platform Arran has caused us to place great tree trunks. Thus, as the slaves push, the platform rolls forward over the trunks. At first, as the trunks emerged from under the back of the platform they rolled backwards killing and maiming many slaves. We can afford the loss of slaves, but replacing the trees proved to take too long. So now a dozen or so slaves pick up the trunk appearing from under the back of the platform and carry it to the front. Thus, we are making good time. By Equinox the obelisk will stand at the top of the mountain and Ra will smile upon us. Ra is great. It is our joy and purpose to serve him forever.

Andrew has fallen asleep at his desk that overlooks the Quad where Georgian facades cast long dark shadows on a manicured lawn. He dreams of golden sand and golden girls and golden treasure in a future elevated far above the mediocrity that incarcerated his youth. Andrew has a future. Oh yes, believe you me, Andrew has a future. Come closing time, the librarian switches off the lights to make the occupants of the library leave. She believes the ancient volumes that line the walls will suffer from an excess of artificial light. It is not within her remit to consider the potential impact of darkness upon examination prospects of undergraduates. Andrew is grateful that at least on the way home the rain will be flowing at him from behind.

I watch them dig their heels into the loose stones
as they struggle to get a grip.

185

He alights from the bus, checks the road name and counts his way up the house numbers to the agreed meeting place. The cherry blossom is coming into flower, all white on this side of the street, all pink on that, some long dead bureaucrat's idea of nature enhanced by subjugation to municipal uniformity. In his pocket his right hand sweats, crushing ten fifty pound notes, the largest amount of money he has ever handled. These new found riches are the legacy of some maiden great aunt he definitely doesn't remember and isn't even certain he ever actually met. Silently he thanks her profusely for her serendipitous death at precisely the right moment to permit the replacement of his uninsured bicycle. As a result of his failure to chain it to the railings, it has met with a premature and watery demise in the Oxford Canal following a rowing club dinner.

"Eight glorious bumps or not, John, I simply do not have time to celebrate your conquests."

Wealth beyond... well not so much beyond the dreams of avarice as beyond his immediate anticipation, results in Andrew driving home from this appointment, having invested in a Morris Minor saloon (J Reg., 1970, rose taupe, one careful owner, full serv. hist., tel. Oxford 42971) at the full advertised price, for Andrew considers it demeaning to asks for discounts. It has just 15,251 miles on the clock

"Absolutely genuine that, son."

faux leather seats

"Don't call 'em plastic, son. They're way easier to keep clean than fabric. You'll be glad you went for faux, son."

and a squeak that seems to emanate from somewhere near the front offside wheel *"That? Oh you don't wanna worry about that – all Morris Minors do that, son. Look at this body work – last for years, that will."*

As he drives happily, if self-consciously, back to his digs in Summertown, Andrew is aware something has changed. The damp bank notes now missing from his pocket? Certainly. The pride he feels sitting behind the wheel of the car? Yes, but something more. Something he can't quite put his finger on. That night he lies in bed, thinking of the naive pride he formerly took in his unremarkable old bicycle, that symbol of student poverty, relieved that he will now arrive at college in the mornings dryer, even if later – parking in Oxford's a pig.

Finally Andrew sleeps. He dreams of pretty legs upon faux leather and champagne picnics lain out under secluded trees; of dark evenings away from streetlamps, where windscreens steam to opacity and warm secret places yield to exploring hands.

At some deeper level than his consciousness knows, Andrew has already begun to wonder what his next car might be.

As the slaves push, the platform rolls forward over the trunks.

It has taken four months; four long months from job offer, to starting work for Caalaka Limited, to fulfilling the probationary period. And three of those months have been an unutterable embarrassment for Andrew.

"Of all the cars I could have chosen – a Morris effin' Minor. Oh, please God no! Anything but that! How could I have been such a nerd, such a complete, unmitigated Wally! I parallel park my shame daily."

But it does have to be said that in Andrew's opinion there is one thing worse than a Morris Minor, and that is a Morris Minor with a torn child seat in the back. It screams 'hard up Family Man' at the top of its high pitched little voice to the whole of the bonus-brandishing, engine-revving, nightly-scoring sales team. Andrew has watched huddled groups of his peers collapse into helpless laughter as he passes them in the corridor, making only the most superficial of pretences that their mirth is induced by something other than him. And just when he thought it could get no worse, he now has to endure the ultimate in corporate shame – the Managing Director's smirk – each time he has the misfortune to arrive in the car park at the same time as the MD's Porsche. He is devastated at the nick name that the MD himself has bestowed upon him: Noddy.

At last! What relief it is to be finally free of the faux pas faux leather of one's discarded immaturity. The offending vehicle has at last been demoted to the diminished status of *Wife's Runabout* ("Oh yes, it's so useful! Clarissa shuttles Paul and Sophie to school in it every morning – she's into retro – and she looks *so* funny turning the crank handle when it won't start."). It has even been reframed to confer an unanticipated benefit: the status of *Two Car Family*, particularly when referred to with studied nonchalance in the presence of lesser mortals, who possess merely a wife, 2.4 children and but a single vehicle. From his newly elevated status of *Driver of Company Car*, Andrew Chakra can at last afford to permit himself, when out of the earshot of the corporate wolf pack, to condescend to just a smidgen of nostalgia for that little car. It was, after all, an Issigonis design and a landmark of British motoring history.

"So long as no one uses the bloody 'N' word."

Now Andrew dreams of olive-skinned Latin lovers, hair strewn carelessly over leather headrests; of shimmering Iberian coastal roads and fireball suns that drop deferentially into the gentle western waves at the approach of conquerors such as he. For it is axiomatic, is it not, that success is a tasteful red pinstripe, black Recaro seats and a Blaupunkt stereo cassette-radio. Success is a Renault Fuego 2.2L hatchback.

> *The sun is high now, but we do not let the slaves stop. It burns their backs as they work, leaving large blisters on their shoulders.*

"One should not, of course, be distracted by one's appointment to the Board even if it does mean a new company car. For one is more, now, than merely a cog within a wheel. One's experience is indispensable to the company as it aspires to list on The FTSE Full Board as Caalaka Group PLC and one feels the weight of responsibility upon one's shoulders."

"I have Lex Motor Leasing on line four for you, Mr. Chakra, do you wish to discuss interior colour options for the E32?"

"Of course, a company vehicle is an invaluable tool, fundamental to the discharge of one's responsibilities. One barely registers how the uninformed might possibly perceive it."

"Cor! Looka that Beemer! Bet that set 'im back a bundle."

"One is uninfluenced by such insignificant matters as status symbols – but Travers really will have to achieve a better shine if he is to retain his position."

We drag the dying away, leaving them for carrion on the mountain side and whip replacements into place from the cages.

"Divorce, Clarissa, is the most ugly of words. Vanessa is my personal assistant. I am the Managing Director of a Public Limited Company, for God's sake. Our relationship is purely professional... Well, she's hardly going to be able to take dictation if she sits in the front with the chauffer, is she? And if you take the trouble to check, you will discover that Rolls Royce Phantoms come with privacy dividers as standard. The mirrored ceiling was a low cost accessory that I had installed as an afterthought to assist with my Transcendental Meditation – you know full well the doctor has instructed me to practice daily to ease my Essential Hypertension... Yes, I will continue paying Sophie's university fees... Yes, if you must you can have The Willows – I'm almost never there anyway... No! You may *not* have the bloody car."

We do not permit the slaves to stop until it is too dark to see.
Many have fallen where they worked.

"I bought it for the view more than anything else. The bridge is stupendous from this angle, particularly at night when it lights up. And the Tower! Sometimes you'd swear you can see Anne Boleyn's barge slipping in through Traitor's Gate. Of course, the allocated parking space under the block is too small to take the Phantom. So I have Travers bring it round in the morning at 9.45 am sharp. That way I can count on being in the office for a ten o'clock start. Well, no one expects the Chairman in before 10.00 am, do they? The evenings? Yes, they can be a bit wearying sometimes. One tires of the perpetual rounds of Royal Openings and exhibitions and concerts. So sometimes I just sit out on the balcony. I listen to the traffic sounds and the water lapping on the river bank. I'm suffering slightly from insomnia, though. So I hit on the idea of another car – not a big one – just a CLK Coupe. I drive out in the small hours, for nothing more than the pleasure of being on the road. I don't go far – just Kings Cross or Soho maybe… just drive around and then come home. I never stop; never talk to anyone."

As the trunks emerged from under the back of the platform they rolled backwards killing and maiming many slaves. We can afford the loss of slaves.

It is exactly two weeks since The News of The World published its four page pictorial spread of alleged impropriety by the Chairman of Caalaka Group PLC, noted FTSE 100 company, with several alleged prostitutes. Well, to be more specific, the night-time aspect of the encounter is not at issue since the cameraman was careful to ensure his images were time and date stamped. Nor, indeed, is the alleged protagonist in the matter now disputing his involvement, even though his first statement did claim he was merely giving a lift home to two young secretaries in his Mercedes sports car after they had worked late. Regrettably, however, this version of events was called into question by the attire of said ladies. Caalaka Group PLC has confirmed through its solicitors that fishnet stockings, high heels and faux fur jackets are not approved day wear for secretarial staff. Their statement further discloses that investigations have been commenced into certain alleged irregularities in the Chairman's office. They will not, however, be more specific as yet.

Thus we are making good time. By Equinox the obelisk will stand at the top of the mountain and Ra will smile upon us.

"He usually goes to Club Gascon. I've watched him cos we're only two doors down, you see. He hesitated outside their door, then changed his mind and walked on here. Well, he wouldn't want to go anywhere too public just at the min, would he? Asked for a quiet table at the back. I didn't say anything to show I recognised him, mind. I feel sorry for the ol' boy, actually. Fancy ending a City career like that – loose women and fingers in the till. Who'd have thought it? He asked me to order for him – just said no fish and a bottle of the best Burgundy on our list. Drank the wine, but didn't touch the food when it came. Never even asked for the bill. Just dropped ten £50 notes on the table. Musta thought he was in Gascon's eh? Me an' Marty had a good night out on that, I don't mind telling you!"

Wait for the sound of the ram's horn – the command to push.

Andrew is alone with his thoughts on this spring evening. He is not sure if he has ever been alone in quite this way before. He has decided to walk the 2.7 miles from the Clerkenwell Road back to Tower Bridge, for the night is warm and his calf muscles make him think of iron. There is no rain driving horizontally towards him from the south up New Bridge Street, nor behind him from the north down Farringdon Road. But there again, neither are the streets lined with municipally-approved cherry blossom. So what will possess his thoughts as he walks, now that his dreams have petrified to obelisks; now that he knows that Ra is great and that it is our joy and purpose to serve him forever?

Images of pretty legs upon faux leather will fade to memories of gurgling babies in torn plastic child seats. The final breath of a mother dying alone of emphysema in an East Finchley council flat will wrap him from behind like an Exhibitioner's gown. Thoughts of Latin lovers will fade like waning fireball suns, as images of lifeless twenty-seven year marriages rise before his face like haunted moons. Hands that explored warm and deep and long ago behind erect privacy screens will now seem somehow less important than corporate governance and the signatures in Chairmen's cheque books.

And still there will be room in his mind for one thought more than any other: the easy theft of neglected, unchained bicycles that can shorten journey times.

Andrew is cycling into the river.

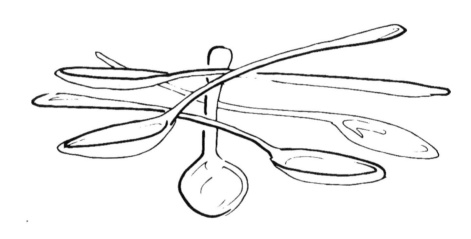

27   I'm Worried About The Spoons

Most of the poor sods in here haven't got a clue where they are – or who they are, for that matter. Virtually all of them have reverted to childhood and think they're five years old again – ironic when you think that the average age actually has to be something over eighty. Not that that makes them easy to manage, mind you. They can still be extremely stubborn – just like small kids I s'pose; violent too, some of 'em. You have to keep your wits about you, cos one or two of 'em lash out without warning. If I had a fiver for every thump I've had working in here, I'd be a rich man. So to look after yourself, you learn some tricks of the trade, see. Get to know which ones are quiet, which ones you need to be wary of. Now, I've got one trade secret that's particularly useful. But if I tell you, you promise not to tell Matron, don't you? Cos Matron's big on that new 'Person Centred Care' thing see, and if she knew what I do when no one's around I reckon it could cost me my job.

Don't you go thinkin' that I'm an abuser though, cos nothing could be further from the truth. I love these ol' dears an' nothing would make me hurt them. But what I do – and I have to admit it's a bit dishonest and not what you might call 'best practice' – what I do, is I pretend I'm a resident!

I can see you're not impressed. But think about it a minute. When the demented old bints are being ordered about by staff they think are in control of them, a lot of 'em get stroppy and do the very opposite of what they're being asked to do. But what I do is get 'em thinking I'm one of them, then it's much easier, isn't it? Instead of sayin' "'Ere Mary, drink this," and then trying to shove a cuppa tea down 'er, I sit down with 'er and drink my tea with 'er. Then she'll drink it down, sweet as a lamb, no questions asked or answered. It's the same when the nurse comes by on the morning drug round. Old 'Enry, he's a right bugger for taking his meds. So what I do, is I get the nurse to give me my blood pressure tablets an' I sit down with 'Enry with a glass of water for each of us. Then the nurse comes along and says 'Right lads, medicine time.' 'Enry, he moans like billio, course. But then I'll say to him, "Come on mate, it's not so bad if we do it together." Then he gets his tranquilisers and I get my blood pressure tabs and it don't feel so bad to him when we take them together, see? The nurses are in on it, course, but they can see the benefit to the patients, so they don't say nothin'. Matron gets to think everything's la-de-person-centred-da, so everyone's happy. An' what could be the harm in that?

Course, this is just a retirement job for me you understand – more like voluntary service than real work. I've got a glitterin' career behind me. Started off with a degree in Sociology. Worked as a social worker for a bit 'til I got hitched. Then when the kids came along an' we needed a few more readies, I retrained as an accountant an' went into the City. Made an absolute fortune after Big Bang – you won't remember that, course, bein' so young. 1987, it was. Everyone into sharp suits and Porches, megabucks bonuses and Docklands flats. Ah, those were the days.

The other staff here ain't all bad. In fact some of them are actually quite nice. I don't mix with them outside of work, you understand – they're not quite in my league. So I just report to Matron at 8.00 am sharp, get given my instructions and get on with the day. But I'm not stand-offish. I pride myself on my ability to mix with people of all classes. Mostly, the people who work here have one clear job – they're care assistants, or they're cleaners, or kitchen assistants or whatever. But me, I'm different. I'm a floater. Or at least that's what I call the job. When I report to Matron at start of shift she deploys me where I'm most needed – always a vital task, of course. This place couldn't run without me. She knows that, I know it, and pretty much everyone else here knows it too. By 9.00 am I might be directing the gardener, or training the chef in the kitchen. At morning drug round I support the nurse. See, lots of the patients here are buggers about taking their meds. But I've got a trade secret that get's 'em to do it every time. You'll never guess what it is. I sit down with the difficult ones – ol' 'Enry, he's usually the worst, an' I pretend I'm a resident! Then I slip the wink to the nurse, and she gives me my blood pressure tablet I gave to her earlier. Then ol' 'Enry, when 'e

194

sees me taking my meds, he's much more willin' to take his, see. It's basic psychology, isn't it? I can see you're impressed with that. Of course I was a clinical psychologist years ago, so I know about this stuff. I wouldn't expect you to understand, but trust me, it works.

At lunchtime Matron usually asks me to have my lunch with the residents. She says there's no one that can calm them like I do. See, she knows, if I have lunch with them, they're much quieter, an' the staff can get them to eat much more easily. I'm quite an influence round 'ere, I can tell you. I don't mind having lunch with them – I've no particular reason to eat in the staff room – most of the other staff are stand-offish buggers anyway. Yesterday, that maintenance man, Bernie, pushed me out of the staff room at coffee time with a "Not *now* Frank, we're having coffee." Well I ask you. How rude can you get? What about me getting a cup of coffee? So I went and sat with the residents an' had my coffee with them. At least they talked to me.

After lunch the residents usually have activities. More often than not, Maisey, the activities organiser, will ask me to help out. She reckons that the job's too much for one person, so she's really grateful for my support an' expertise. See, she knows I was an entertainer before I retired. I don't make a big deal out of this, but I was in the Royal Variety Performance in '92. I've still got a picture of me shaking hands with the Queen mother after the show. Ah, those were the days. The limelight an' the music an' the applause… and the women… I could tell you some stories about the times I had when I was in show business.

When activities are over I'm generally drafted in by the kitchen to help with the tea round. Course some of the resident's aren't too good about drinking their tea, and it's medically essential that they have sufficient fluids. But I've got a trick up my sleeve that usually gets it down 'em. Want me to tell you what it is? Well, all I do is, I sit with them an' drink a cuppa with them! Then, cos they think I'm one of them, they'll drink the tea down, quiet as lambs! Simple, ain't it? But the best solutions to problems often are the simplest ones. I can see you're impressed. But then I was big on problem solving when I was an international management consultant.

195

After activities, most of 'em will doze off in the lounge for a bit, so that leaves me free to carry out one of my most important jobs. Well, it's more of a project than a job, cos I been workin' on it for several months now. Matron's asked me to take a full inventory of the cutlery each day, cos she's worried we might have a thief on the premises. She says cutlery's so easy to steal, and I can see she's got a point. At the moment we don't know if it's an intruder, somehow entering for the purpose or whether it's someone on the inside. But I'm keeping my eyes peeled I can tell you. Course Matron's appointed me to the task on account of my experience with the Flying Squad. She knows how fortunate she is to have someone of my calibre on the staff. But I have to tell you, I'm worried about the spoons. Yesterday I counted them; forty-seven pudding spoons and twenty-three tea spoons. This afternoon we're down to forty-one pudding spoons, but the number of tea spoons is actually up to twenty-nine! So now I can see what's going on. The criminal is bringin' in tea spoons and swappin' 'em for dessert spoons. Oh, he's a clever one alright, but not clever enough for me. An' now I know his game, I'll be on the lookout. I've reported my preliminary findings to Matron and she's asked me to write her a report on the matter. I got really good on report writing when I was an Inspector at Ofsted. Won't be long now an' I'll have 'im.

Come supper time I'm generally needed in the kitchen again. I've told Matron that chef's over-working the kitchen assistants, and she's asked if I've nothing on in the evenings if I wouldn't mind lending a hand to take the pressure off, like. Well, there's no one waiting for me at home, so I thought, 'Why not?' an' I've been helpin' regular in the kitchen ever since. Mind, no one's said anything about payment. I reckon it's about time I raised that one with administrator, so maybe that will be tomorrow's job.

By the evening, Matron's usually gone home and been replaced by her deputy. Florence her name is, but we all call her Flo. Go with the Flo, we say! But she doesn't mind a bit of teasin' from the staff. Actually, she had a word with me a while back. Called me back, just as I was about to go out of the door on my way home actually. It was, "Oh, Frank, could you come here a moment please?" So I went over to her wondering if I'd done

196

summin' wrong – I was thinkin' maybe someone had spilled the beans over my pretending to be a resident. I was all set to justify myself, when she said summin' completely unexpected. "Frank," she says, "I really need to ask you for your help."

"Really?" I says. "How can I help?"

She says, "Well, it's like this. You having been a famous trainer an' all, Matron an' I were wondering if you could help us out with staff trainin'."

"Well, certainly," I says, "'what do you need me to do?"

"Well," she says, "we've been gettin' a lot of new staff on the evenin' and night shifts recently, an' the problem is they're inexperienced."

"'Ah," I says, "I'm getting' yer drift. Want me to show 'em the ropes, do ya?"

"Well," she says, "in a way, yes. But we want you to do it in a particular way, Frank, so as to make it as realistic for 'em as possible."

"I'm listening," I says.

"What we'd like you to do, Frank," she says, "is to do some role play for 'em."

"Role play?" I asks, not quite followin' what she means.

"Yes, role play," she says. "We'd like you to role play bein' a resident for us, in the evenings and at night. The new staff aren't gettin' the experience they need, see, so we was wonderin' if you could, like, act out the part of bein' a resident."

"Ah," I says, "now I'm gettin' yer drift. You wants me to act out bein' a resident, so they gets to practice on me. An' that would be on account of you knowin' that I was a famous Shakespearian actor before I came to work here?"

"*Exactly*, Frank," she says. "That's exactly what I mean. Are you up for it?"

"Not 'arf," I says. "'Bin a while since I trod the boards. If you need an actor, Flo, I'm yer man. When would you like me to start?"

"Well," she says, "we was wonderin' if you could start this evenin', an' stay over to help train the night staff. We've got a room you can stay in and we've sent out for some of your personal stuff for you already. Like to come an' see?"

"Sure," I says, an' she takes me down to this little room at the end of the corridor. An' sure enough, she's right. There's a box on the wall outside the room with pictures in, an' they look familiar. When I squint up real close, I can see that it's me in one of 'em, an' if I'm not mistaken, it was taken on Morecombe beach. There's a woman standin' next to me... an' I'm thinkin'... thinkin' I ought to know who she is.

"Do you recognise the picture, Frank?" Flo says, but I can't quite remember. So we go into the room, and sure enough, someone's been round to my house and got my pyjamas an' put 'em out for me on the bed. An' get this – Flo helps me out of my clothes and into my pyjamas.

"So you're takin' this role play an' trainin' really seriously, then?" I says.

"We certainly are, Frank," Flo says, "an' we're really, really glad of the help of a true expert like you. But just one thing, Frank. Do you think, if I leave the bathroom door open and the light on, you can remember to use the toilet, and not pee in the waste basket tonight? We don't need quite *that* much realism in the training!"

Well, I giggle at the thought of that. "Course I can, Flo," I say. "From the way you're talkin' anyone would think I 'ad senile dementia!"

She's only just shut the door and put the light off when I suddenly remember! I leap out of bed an' make straight for the door, callin' after her.

"Flo," I calls, "Flo! I've forgotten to give Matron me report about the spoons. I'm really worried about the spoons!"

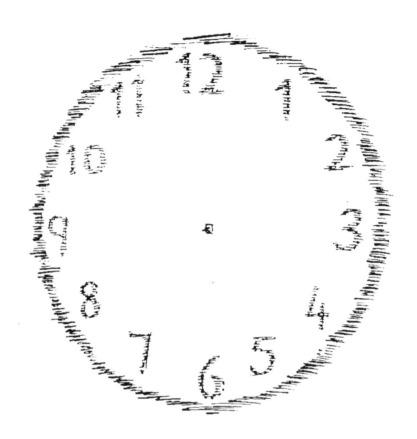

28   Escape Velocity

From the armchair he can't see the clock through his cataracts. He can hear it ticking though. Nothing wrong with his hearing. He senses the time; knows by intuition it's five to six. Time for Marty's supper. Bony hands shiver down the threadbare fabric of the chair arms. Deep blue veins protrude as his fingers trace the indentations made by the same action repeated countlessly over the years. He leans forward, braces, pushes down, his arms shaking as he starts to rise. He reaches escape velocity; stands in an octogenarian parody of the vertical. Breathing deeply, he shuffles seven slow steps to the kitchen. Lunch remains untouched where Sadie left it for him. Food is too much trouble now. But Marty… Marty needs his supper. He stands before the cupboard, and reaches for the door with shaking hand. "Careful now. You're not seventy-five anymore." He draws the door slowly open and reaches for the packet. As he stoops, one hand on the kitchen worktop steadies him while he pours dried food into the aluminium bowl on the floor. He smiles as it rattles. Marty always comes when he hears that.

"Marty… suppertime."

He stands bending over the bowl waiting for the dog to snuffle his hand before he starts eating.

Then the tsunami comes. Full force, no warning, washing over him.

Still leaning over the bowl, he emits a long, low moan. Then in a faltering voice he whispers, "Why couldn't I have gone first?"

29   Rainbow

"Look at the rainbow," said Mummy, pointing into the sky. "See the pretty colours. There's a pot of gold at the end of the rainbow, you know." I believed her, taking solemn note, for I was three.

"Look at the rainbow," said teacher. "It is made of light. You can remember the colours by the mnemonic, Richard of York gave battle in vain. Some say there is a pot of gold at the end of the rainbow." But I knew better. And I was hurt, wounded, to discover that teachers lie, so I refused to believe. I disdained stories of leprechauns counting gold into pots as fantasy, for I was seven.

"Look at the rainbow," said my first girlfriend. We were sitting on the hill under the old oak tree and I had just stolen a kiss. "It's beautiful. And there's a pot of gold at the end of it." I pretended to believe her, for she was lovely and I wanted her so much. We did not last – she said I went too fast for her, for I was seventeen.

"Look at the rainbow," said my fellow travellers as we waited in long queues, briefcases in hand, at the ticket machines, that we might ride the train to our offices in the city. "There's a pot of gold at the end of that, so what are we doing here?" they grumbled, needing to believe. At our offices we sat in rows in front of VDUs and wound the truth into enticing misrepresentations for those who had convinced themselves that there are indeed pots of gold at the ends of rainbows. And I too wanted to believe in those pots of gold, since I struggled with the mortgage and the school fees, for I was thirty-five.

"Look at the rainbow," said my wife, as we sat in the row boat in the middle of the lake, holding hands on this, our celebratory retirement trip. "Do you think there's a pot of gold at the end of it?" I thought carefully. "Yes," I replied truthfully, for at that moment I did. I needed desperately to believe I would find that pot of gold before it was too late, for I was sixty-five.

"Look at the rainbow," they said, as they stood outside the crematorium. "See the pretty colours. You can remember the colours by the mnemonic, Richard of York gave battle in vain. It's beautiful. And there's a pot of gold at the end of it, so what are we doing here?" they asked themselves.

I stood with my angel and watched them from a safe distance. They were not supposed to see us, there being much that is told to the dead that the living should not know. I turned to my angel and asked, "Is there really a pot of gold at the end of the rainbow?"

My angel smiled at me and replied, "It all depends on which end of the rainbow you're looking."

30   Circling The Moon

So you landed at Bird and when they opened the door you felt like the heat was going to suck you out of the plane. You hung back behind the steward's politely obstructive arm while Upper Class filed out, smug superiority written over every face. Then it was your turn to feel richer-than-thou as he stood back to let you exit, and smiled a deferential 'goodbye' while Economy stood behind him, panting for freedom. You walked down the aircraft steps into the Caribbean sunshine as the sound of the steel band wafted over the tarmac to welcome you, just as it had done thirty-three years before.

But that was only nine years after Independence and it had all changed – even the name of the airport had changed. Back then it was called Cool Edge or maybe Coolidge or some such. And in those days it was you panting to get out of economy with your mates and down onto those unbelievable white sands you'd read about. And when the four of you, taking a year out to see the world before university, managed to settle the argument over who was to pay the taxi, you asked the driver to take you to the beach that had the prettiest girls on the island. So he said you must want Dickenson Bay and when you said you liked the sound of the 'Dick' part but you weren't so keen on getting a 'son' out of it, it raised a laugh from your mates. And if you'd known what was coming, then you'd likely have got out of the taxi and back onto the next flight to anywhere. But you didn't know and you couldn't know so you just flowed with that new-wine-in-old-bottles exuberance of young men grasping hold of a world they know for a fact will deliver them everything they dream of. When you got to Dickenson, all four of you raced down onto that soft white sand, past that all important market stall, leaping and whooping and swinging your Black Sabbath and T-Rex t-shirts over your heads.

And without stopping you ran headlong into the white surf and the warm petral water and swam out a few yards to lie on your back looking up at the perfect blue sky, thinking it was the nearest place to paradise you'd ever been.

You hadn't seen her then. But she'd seen you.

You passed those days lying in the sun and watching the bikini-clad tourist girls slide past, up the sand and back down again until they were sure that you and every other vaguely virile male on the beach were half erect or better at the sight of them. And you passed the nights in the nightclubs of the beachside hotels or in St John's where the same girls, or girls just like them, gyrated to steel bands and rock bands and poured out onto the street, still dancing, with rum punches in hand and boyfriends glued to their hips. And it seemed that if you so much as looked sideways at anyone with good tits or a pretty face, the boyfriends would be on you in an instant, demanding to know what your game was, threatening you with Christ-knows-what, and dispatching you, tail between your legs, back to Dickenson, where you'd wank your way to a lonely sunrise.

And still you hadn't noticed her, standing behind a makeshift stall every day at the top of the beach, hidden away amongst the t-shirts and dresses and blouses that she sold to the holiday makers. And still you hadn't seen her looking at you, barely taking her eyes off you except to serve a customer, for the whole of the eleven days you'd spent on the beach. Chances are if someone hadn't stolen your one good t-shirt while you slept you'd never have had cause to go to her beach stall to buy a new one with money you didn't want to afford. Even then you're not sure you'd have really noticed her if it hadn't been for the way she fixed her eyes on you, and the shy sideways smile she gave you. And then there was the slow, slow way she poured your change carefully from her right hand into your left palm as she supported it with her own left hand so as to prolong that first touch as long as possible, gripping your gaze desperately until you understood precisely what she wasn't saying. It was only at that moment that you finally got the point and asked her name and she answered in a shy whisper, 'Ruth.' And that was the turning point. That was when everything became different. And it became different because of the Rules.

You'd first become aware of the Rules as soon as you went to school. In Mrs. Baker's reception class, you had dutifully beaten on tambourine and xylophone while singing happily out of key to a badly tuned piano that 'the ink was black and the page was white.' And when you went home and sang your new song to Mummy and Daddy, they nodded and smiled approvingly to hear how 'together you were going to learn to read and write.' But you became uneasy when you got to the part that said 'a child is black, a child is white' and the nods and smiles became a little less enthusiastic and you thought you must be singing the words wrong even though you remembered them from class. And by the time you reached the end where it said 'now the child must understand that this is the law of all the land,' Daddy had left the room and Mummy wasn't smiling any more. And when you asked if you'd done something bad Mummy said 'No, of course not, Darling' and that it was a lovely song and everyone should learn to sing it. But that night when you'd gone to bed you heard loud voices downstairs. The next day you were sent to school with a note. The next week Daddy came to see Mrs. Baker. The week after that you started at a new school and you thought you must have done something really, really bad and you cried because you hadn't meant to be bad. But no one ever told you what you'd done and you didn't know why you had had to change schools, you just knew you were a bad, bad boy and you had to be more careful next time.

As you grew older your understanding of the Rules grew with you. You came to realise that there were bad programmes on TV and that Daddy turned them off. You weren't to talk about them, even if it was 'Love Thy Neighbour,' and all your friends were talking about it in school the next morning.

You remembered when you finally knew you understood the Rules perfectly. You were twelve and out with Dad one morning, when coming towards you up the street were a black man and a white woman and the woman was pushing a push chair with a baby in it that was a bit black and a bit white and you thought that was called 'half-caste.' When Dad crossed the street without warning you weren't surprised, because you knew it was in the Rules for him to do so. And you also knew it was in the Rules that you weren't supposed to ask him about it. It was only later when you were thinking about it that you'd realised you had come to learn the Rules without anyone ever saying what they were. But now you just knew them by heart.

Later, in Science, you learned about a process called osmosis.

It was ok, it really was, because at nineteen Ruth had already had a lifetime of looking after herself and everyone else and just one more child wouldn't make any difference at all.

It was ten years since her mother had died; ten years since she was left to look after four brothers and sisters aged from four to seven; ten years since she learned to feed the family on the erratic next-to-nothing money Dadda was willing to give her when he was sober. School had been out of the question, of course, so she'd taught herself what she could from borrowed books by lamplight when the children were in bed and Dadda was busy upending beer bottles and sliding his hand up loose women's skirts in a dark corner of some dark bar. From the books she'd learned enough to dream of more life than her obligations to a dependent family would ever permit. On the odd occasions that she could find some free time she would go to the airport at St John's and watch the flights arriving and leaving, watch their cargo of white tourists disembarking and re-embarking and wonder what it must be like to afford a holiday. Or if there was no time to go to the airport she would stand on the hill overlooking Half Moon Bay and wait for the catamarans, their sails full of wind, their decks full of holidaymakers, circle past from the north until they disappeared behind the headland to the southwest, always ending up where they started and changing nothing, driven by a wind they could follow but could never control, making circles round the moon, as Ruth thought of it.

At fifteen she'd discovered that money could be had from the tourists for baskets and toys that she could weave from palm fronds that cost nothing. And since her youngest brother was now nine and better able to look after himself, Ruth set herself to the noble art of parting white people, burned lobster-red by the unforgiving sub-tropical sun, from as many of their green dollars as possible – a skill at which she proved to be particularly adept. From woven trinkets she moved on to small items of jewellery and eventually to a stall at Dickenson. At first the other vendors had tried to shoo her away, but for those determined enough to withstand the pecking of the established traders, eventually the opposition died out. If her role as parent from the age of nine had taught her anything it was patience and determination. So she shrugged off the sarcasm and the occasional half-hearted sabotage attempt on her stall until eventually the opposition fell silent. Within a year she was accepted as a trader herself and after a second had one of the best looking stalls on the beach, selling trinkets and toys and t-shirts and dresses.

About that time she'd been surprised to find herself the subject of male attention for the first time, wondering what on earth it could be that brought the boys buzzing round her stall like sand flies. Occasionally one would press his attentions onto her too far and she'd push him away hard, or cry out for help, whereupon a bevy of wide-girthed middle aged female traders in long skirts and headscarves would surround her stall and drive the unwanted intruder back with derision and an occasional balled fist. Accordingly, male attention, in Ruth's mind, became a matter at best of irritation and at worst fear. But that was before David had come.

She'd not known his name then. She'd seen him arrive at the beach with his friends one afternoon when the sun was hot and thought anyone sensible who had a choice would be sitting in the shade of the bar with a beer cold enough to make condensation run down the outside of the glass. She'd noticed them initially for their stupidity – giggling immaturely and bumping her stall as they ran down to the water, rushing as if the sea wouldn't still be there tomorrow. She'd watched the blond one, the one with legs and arms a bit too long for his torso and a beard unusually full for a boy his age, as he came and went over the next few days. She could see he was making the beach his temporary home before moving off to some place Ruth could barely dream of and could never aspire to go. She would toss her head back and tell herself it was nothing to her as he eyed the bikini-clad white girls parading their bodies shamefully along the beach, trying to look as if they didn't know every man's eye was on them. She'd watched as he rinsed his horrible black t-shirt – the one with the awful demon motif on it – under the beach tap and thought about how much better he'd look in one of hers. When she found herself returning to the beach each evening after trading hours she first convinced herself she was only being sensible in making sure nothing bad happened to her pitch for as long as these foolish young Englishmen insisted on camping out on her stretch of sand. But when she stayed awake into the night awaiting their return, and when she felt her heart beat faster as she heard them approaching, and when she felt angry and betrayed and cheated on when they staggered back, drunk and singing, and the blond one had his arm around a girl, that was when it started to get difficult to ignore what was happening to her. And when, the following night, she stole the horrible black t-shirt while the blond boy slept, she couldn't pretend any longer.

After you'd extricated yourself from the grip of that long, meaningful gaze, you made your way back to your mates further up the beach, but you couldn't help looking repeatedly back. And each time you did, there she was, standing by the t-shirt stall watching you, never taking her eyes off you, telling you with that incessant stare how much she wanted you and that she was yours whenever you decided to take up the offer. She was nothing special to look at. There was no particular attraction in her round, even face, no distinctive poise about her bearing or advantage of height to bestow elegance upon her. She was just an ordinary black girl, braided hair, full breasts, short in the leg with a waist line that was already beginning to prophesy expansion in middle age. Mercifully, your mates hadn't seen the exchange, so there was no teasing or goading or mockery and you had the rest of the morning to collect your thoughts. So when Henry had gone off with the girl he brought back with him last night – the one you put your arm round momentarily until he jabbed you in the kidneys to warn you off – and when Jamie and Frank had ambled away to see if they could blag a ride on a catamaran, you'd made an excuse and stayed behind. When there was no bravado and no one egging you on, you had the chance, for once, to do exactly what you wanted to, to sail your own boat to exactly where you chose to go. And you decided right there and then that your destiny didn't include a black Antiguan girl called Ruth, because when all the bluff and bravado of nineteen-year-olds was stripped away, underneath it all you thought of yourself as fundamentally one of the good guys and hurting people and walking away wasn't who you wanted to be. So no, there was going to be no taking advantage, no quick shag and jetting off to your next scheduled destination. You decided then and there that when Henry and Jamie and Frank came back you'd tell them you'd had enough of Antigua and you wanted to move on. And just to make sure the point was clearly made, you started packing up your rucksack. You were just zipping up the top with a decisive pull that told the world you absolutely meant what you said, when from behind you she spoke.

"I thought you might like a drink," she said. For all the years that have passed, you can still hear it; that deep Caribbean voice; the voice that sounded like tropical waterfalls and felt like the sun on your back; the soft, shy voice that made you realise that the only thing you knew was what you did not know. And for some unfathomable reason you didn't need to turn round to know that she held a can of chilled beer in her outstretched hand, even if you didn't know that she'd gone to the bar to buy it with the money you'd given her for the t-shirt. But you had to turn round, you couldn't not turn round, couldn't just carry on with what you were doing, pretending you hadn't heard. And as you did turn, there she was, exactly as you knew she would be, holding out the beer, only that in the other hand she held one for herself as well. And in that turning, you'd let her breech your defences, hadn't you? And when you reached out for the beer and said "Thank you," because you'd accepted something from her, you'd put her in control. That gave her the opportunity to steer where all this was going, even though later she told you there was no way to control any of it, only the wind to follow that would bring you both back to where you started, only the circles round the moon.

You sat side by side on the sand, she a little distance from you to start with, watching the waves caress the beach, drinking the chilled beer and saying nothing, because there was nothing that needed to be said. But during the conversation that you weren't having, there was the compulsion to touch and be closer and you knew she wanted it just as you wanted it. So you moved nearer to her until your hips were touching and your knees were touching and your feet were touching. And then it was the most natural thing in the world to reach out your hand and let it fall gently on the soft inner side of her thigh – not that you were coming on to her, not that you wanted to touch her up or shag her, because those thoughts just weren't there. There was simply the need to be closer.

It didn't happen the way she planned it to. Though the t-shirt she stole was scuffed and torn, Ruth was overwhelmed with guilt for taking it and dropping it into one of the refuse bins behind the beach bar. So when he came to her stall to buy a replacement, though her heart beat so hard it hurt, it was as much out of shame as excitement. And when he paid her with a large Caribbean Dollar note, she carefully counted out the exact change and poured it into his hand, to ensure she took nothing else from him that was not hers to take. Their eyes had met of course, just like in the movies she very occasionally could afford to see in St John's, but as she looked at him all she could think of was that she'd done him wrong, put him to unnecessary expense. And when he had asked her name she could give no more response than a one word answer, could find nothing inside herself to prolong the conversation, so overcome was she with her own boldness and dishonesty and manipulation. And when he had smiled and walked away an empty retribution sweep over her, chastising her for her wrongdoing, his departure punishing her so fittingly for her crime. She chided herself for her dishonesty and her presumptuousness and her foolish hope that he might have reason to take interest in her. She stood, watching him, in hope that he might turn around and worried that if he did he would see the tears in her eyes. But he was too far away to see the tears in her eyes and too far away for her to reach out to and too far away for her to love. And still the sense of guilt for the only materially dishonest act of her life plied upon her, and pressed her down, so that she missed several of the tourists that looked in on her stall and might easily have been persuaded to do business with her.

"Enough," she eventually said to herself, knowing that there would be no relief until she had compensated him for the deprivation of the t-shirt. And thus it was that the barman at the beach bar was amazed to find Ruth, frugal, careful Ruth, serious, responsible Ruth, standing in front of him asking for two chilled beers. He was not to know that their price was almost exactly the same as that of the t-shirt she had sold to David whom she did not yet know as David. 'I will take him the two beers and leave them with him without speaking,' she determined. As she carried them up the beach they chilled her hands to discomfort. But as she reached his camp and saw he was packing to leave, her guilt was exceed by her fear of losing what she had only just found and had never possessed, and she had to speak. "I thought you might like a drink," she said, holding out just one of the beers. And as he turned to face her and thank her, she found just enough confidence to sit where he motioned that she should, a respectful foot and a half away from him. As they sat side by side, silently watching the waves slide up the beach he moved closer to her so that she felt anxious and uncomfortable and excited and wanted. And when his hip touched her hip and his knee touched her knee and his foot touched her foot she said nothing. And when his hand slipped down to caress the inner side of her thigh, she wanted nothing but to sit silently with him, watching the surf.

Ruth had no way of knowing how long they had sat there, apart from the movement of the sun and the afternoon shadows it was casting longer and longer upon the beach. Eventually, though, she knew there was something else she wanted; something she wanted to show him and share with him. Without looking at him and without turning to him, "I would like to show you my cats," she said.

Harry had never thought of himself as an ambitious man. After all, when he was a kid the whole family had been offered the chance to leave the island – back in '69 it was, a couple o' years after Independence, when Pappa had discovered there was work to be had in London as a bus conductor. Pappa'd thought he'd look mighty fine in one of those dark blue peaked caps he'd seen in the recruiting brochure, rolling tickets for those fine English people that rode the bus to work every morning. But Mamma, she didn't feel right about it. Said it didn't 'witness with her spirit' and she'd had no word from the Lord that they was to go. Anyway, she said, a man needed to really know he was makin' the right move afore he left an island with a different beach for every day of the year, and wasn't that paradise enough for anyone? So the idea had been dropped, the family had stayed and Harry had grown up in Antigua.

"Smilin,' always smilin'," Mamma used to say of him. "That boy always smilin'. Smilin' Harry blessed wid the happiness of the Lord Hisself, Praise His Holy Name." And for his blessed state of happiness she would call upon him to do good works in thanks and praise to her God. Ever obliging, Harry would follow her instructions, distributing bibles in St John's on a Saturday morning, collecting for the missionaries of Africa in the afternoon and taking discarded school books to the young girl next door in the evenings, the one who was struggling to raise her brothers and sisters and still give herself some kind of education. And sometimes Harry would stand outside her ramshackled house, such a contrast to his own, and watch through the window as she studied by lamplight. Then he would whisper a prayer to a god he was not sure existed in thanks that she was not his responsibility.

While God graciously received Mamma's praises in the Elim Pentecostal Church each Sunday, Smiling Harry would walk the beaches, one each week, to find out if it really was true that the Island had a beach for every day of the year. He pursued his objective faithfully, walked and counted twenty-nine beaches until, just after his tenth birthday, they'd done long division in school and he'd dauntingly calculated it would take him almost seven years to complete his self-appointed task. At that moment he'd decided to accept Mamma's estimate. However, by then it was, so to speak, too late. For Smiling Harry had already walked the ten miles from Willikies, climbed a hill on the south eastern side of the island and seen a sight that made him quite certain there really was a God, just as Mamma had always said.

From where he looked down, the lush vegetation fell away beneath a cloudless cerulean sky for perhaps two miles until it reached a bay shaped like a crescent moon. There, a strip of coral pink sand seemed to open its arms to welcome the white foamy surf that rolled and tumbled towards it. To the southern half of the crescent stood what he assumed to be a small hotel. To the northern end, there was nothing; nothing but sand and surf and the warm sunshine sparkling on the surface of the impossibly turquoise water; nothing but a nearly disused car park with rough stone steps down onto the beach and a tumbled down wooden bar.

It was at that moment that Harry knew two things. First, that he would never leave this island. Second, that if it was to be within his power, when he grew up he would live and work in this bay.

When he graduated school he portered at the airport, waited table at English Harbour and worked road construction around St John's whenever the Government was willing to spend the money. And never mind if friends called him to drink at the bar and stop working so hard, or the girls looked at him with inviting eyes or shook their hips suggestively as they passed him. Smiling Harry heeded none of them. "What you need all dis money for, Harry?" Mamma would ask. "Don' you forget, St Paul say Money is d'root of all evil an' you be going to the Devil if you love it too much." But to Harry the money was no more than a necessary step on the road to Half Moon Bay. By the time he was twenty-two, he had enough set aside to buy a small area of land around the bar and the right to use the road that led down to it. It was to be another two years of portering and waiting table and road construction before he had saved enough to rebuild the bar until finally, in 1974, Smiling Harry's opened for business.

Well, of all the things to break the perfect moment! You weren't sure you'd heard her correctly, so you asked her to repeat. "I would like to show you my cats," she said again.

"Your cats?" you questioned incredulously, still believing you must have misheard her.

"Yes. My cats," she repeated. "My sea cats, circling the moon."

And then you knew that one of you must be suffering from excessive exposure to the sun. But you really weren't quite sure which, so you thought you'd better go along with her.

"Come with me," she said, standing up. And you walked with her, slipping your hand into hers and not caring what anyone thought, back to her stall, where she locked up for the night. Then she took you to where she parked her scooter and motioned for you to get on the back. Down into St John's she drove you, past the brightly coloured Anglican churches and Pentecostal churches, past the innumerable makeshift billboards advertising reflexology or massage or spiritual consultation and out on Factory Road towards Willikies. Here the signs of salvation yielded to a mishmash of

217

chain linked fences dividing residential plots, their houses broken and barely habitable or brightly painted and proudly maintained, the gardens a jungle of weeds or carefully tended, until the shanty town finally gave way to a thirsty greenery that lusted after the rains that were yet to come. Down on to Half Moon Bay she drove, where she killed the two stroke engine just as the light was beginning to fade. She took your hand again and walked you down to a beach bar called Smiling Harry's where the barman, who was all of six foot four and built with it, was just closing up. He greeted her warmly, merely glancing at you, a look of some suspicion in his eyes. Then she insisted on buying you another beer, even though you didn't really want it. And you sat, the two of you, at an old rickety wooden trestle table, one can of beer between you, looking out into the bay until she grabbed your hand and said, "Look, a cat," pointing out into the water. Your eyes scanned the waves repeatedly, looking everywhere for some unfortunate furry animal that might have been swept out into the bay, but you could see none. And she gripped onto your arm and said, "No, look there! *The boat!*" And you looked where she was pointing, right out into the bay, further out than you'd be comfortable swimming, until at last you saw what she saw and understood what she meant. You peered through the rapidly disappearing daylight to see the silhouette of a catamaran as it slipped silently round the bay and disappeared behind the tip of the southern headland.

"Now I understand!" you said, laughing.

But she looked at you with dark serious eyes and shook her head and said, "No, you do not understand. You only see, you do not understand."

And in that moment you knew she was right – that you were nineteen and just testing the water of life with a cautious toe before committing yourself and you knew that though you saw, you did not understand. And you knew that though she couldn't have been any older than you, this girl who even now didn't know your name yet had taken control of your heart, this girl could see and could understand in a way that you could not; that in a way you could not yet explain to yourself, this girl was your beginning and your end and all of the journey in between. So you looked at her with eyes more honest than you'd ever looked at anyone ever before and you implored her: "Teach me."

Then she smiled at you and took your hand and led you down on the pink sand that was turning to grey in the falling twilight. You left your sandals at the foot of some stone steps and walked together down to the water's edge where the sea swept over your feet and the soft wet sand seeped up between your toes. Then, acknowledging that there was a hotel and lights and tourists to your right you turned away, turned to the north, seeing your way by the starlight as the last of the daylight sighed and died. Hand in hand you walked up the beach through the surf, listening to the waves breaking on the shore, until you were well away from the last few people on the beach. As you came to the northern end of the crescent you knew, and you knew that she knew, that it was time. She led you up the beach to a place where the bushes swayed over the sand and you lay with her, sliding your arms under her back and kissing her face until she turned her lips towards you. Then you kissed those lips as if you'd never kissed another girl before and as if you never wanted to kiss another again for all the days that you would live. And as you kissed her she slid her hands down inside your shorts, pushing them down your thighs. Then using her feet, she pushed them further, until she'd removed them from your legs entirely, making you naked from the waist down. But even though you knew what she wanted and you wanted it too, you were too shy, or too overwhelmed with the moment to do more until she slipped her hand between your thighs and guided your cock towards her open legs. And then you weren't shy or overwhelmed any more.

Later, as you both lay back looking up at the stars, you asked her about the catamarans. Why were they important to her? What was it about them that attracted her? And she told you how they carried the tourists that came to the island, always clockwise, always following the prevailing winds, able to move in the flow of the wind yet never able to move against it; how they carried the hopes and dreams of each person aboard, how they made people feel that they had arrived where they wanted to be and that they had everything they could possibly want. Yet in truth all they could do was go on sailing round the island, ending up back where they came from and that meant that their end was there, right there, in their beginning, at the place they had started. And because for those that rode the cats nothing had changed on their return, that meant that they had gained nothing and that they knew nothing. And right where you were, at Half Moon Bay, all they could do was sail past, circling the moon. And you told her you thought you understood, not realising that it would be years before you truly did.

Though she knew he had not understood, he came willingly – a first act of trust that she did not feel she deserved. For the first time in her life she'd shut the stall early, asking the neighbouring trader to look over it for her. She'd taken him out to Half Moon Bay on her little moped, deliberately passing her own home and Harry's without comment, concentrating on the feeling of his arms around her from behind as she drove. When they'd arrived at Smiling Harry's Bar she'd looked directly at Harry, as if to tell him not to interfere. So Harry, clearly against his real inclinations, just served her with a beer that he knew was for the man and that he knew she could not afford, saying nothing, but worrying lest she came to harm. Later she had taken him down onto the beach and they'd walked away to her special place where she liked to sit and watch the sun go down. And when the last of the daylight had gone she had taken him in her arms and, despite his reticence, taken him inside herself – the first man to whom she had entrusted her body – the only one, as far as she was concerned, that she would ever do this with. And afterwards they had lain in the darkness, and she had tried to explain, with a wisdom beyond her bodily years, a knowledge born of past lives, or genetic memory, or collective unconscious, how few choices there really were and how much people fool themselves into believing they are in control of their lives. But he had not understood. She had not expected him to.

Afterwards, all through the fall months of the northern continents, when the cold winds blew the tourists to the island in their droves, they had come to the bay at the end of each day. She took to shutting up the stall early to enable them to ride over in the daylight. David, as she had come to know him to be named, would buy the beers from Harry and they would sit at the trestle table looking out to see as sunset threw fire across the sky. As the days passed Harry watched David's relationship with Ruth deepen. Then he came first to accept, and finally to like David.

Harry would tower over him as he brought the beers. "Why you sittin' so still, Mon?" Harry enquired as David sat silently by Ruth one afternoon, looking out to sea. "You made a nitro-glycerine or sumthin'?" Then he roared at his own joke and took to calling David 'Nitro,' a name of which David heartily approved, but knew, like everything here, belonged to the island and not to him.

At home, or so the newspaper headlines told you, they were having a winter of discontent, consisting of three day working weeks, power cuts and strikes. But you had no particular need to go home anyway. Jamie and Frank and Henry had moved on, heartily pissed off at your preoccupation with "that black girl" as they insisted on calling her – at least that's what they called her in your presence. So you'd allowed yourself to sink slowly into that famous Caribbean nonchalance, not caring too much what the world did or what the day did. You found yourself work here and there, cleaning a bar in the morning, preparing vegetables in a hotel kitchen during an afternoon – whatever you could find until Ruth was ready to shut up shop. And yes, though you hated to admit it to yourself, you'd even started to write poetry when there was nothing else to do – a sign of a complete and utter nutcase as far as you were concerned at that time. But what the hell, you were never going to let anyone else know about it, let alone read it, so what did it matter?

As Ruth slowly revealed more of her life to you, you would find ways of slipping cash to her without making much of it. She, for her part, would accept the money and the consideration gratefully, saying nothing. Each afternoon you'd balance precariously on the back of her moped, clearly designed without a passenger in mind, and slip your arms around her waist for pleasure as much as for stability as she guided the little vehicle down to Half Moon Bay. Each twilight you'd arrive at Harry's a few minutes before closing and without your asking he would pull out two cold beers and two sandwiches, waving your hand away when you tried to pay him saying "No money, Nitro, no money. You jus' look after dat girl – she mada gold, man – she precious."

Then you'd sit with her at the trestle table looking out into the bay, waiting for the catamarans to make their twilight run around the island. And as the darkness fell she would lead you once more down to her special place on the beach, the place that was now special to you too, where she would open her heart and her body to you and you would make love by starlight.

You had no way of knowing, no way of anticipating. That day, a Saturday, when she came to you at Dickenson looking troubled, when you asked her what was wrong, she did not reply. She just took you by the hand like it was any other day and led you to the moped and drove you to Half Moon where Harry served you beer and sandwiches just like it was any other day, though something told you it wasn't like any other day. And when the darkness fell she led you down onto the beach and to your special place, still saying nothing. And you knew, could tell, could feel in the racing of her heart and the grip of her hand on yours that this was different. That night she made love to you with a passion, a fire that you had not known in her before, as if by the burning of that fire and the thrusting of her body under you and upon you and in front of you, she could outrun the coming light of day. But the world turned and the night passed and the daylight came. And as the first grey streaks of dawn sketched silhouettes on the beach, she told you; told you that this was the last time; that your shared time had run out of time and that it was time for you to leave.

Then came angry words and violent eyes and a turning away.

Then came weeping, because you knew, even though you did not want to know.

Then came hugging until finally there came acceptance; a sullen acceptance, devoid of reconciliation that faced the hated truth that you could not change the world or outrun it and you could not change her mind or even steer it. For like the cats, and the tourists they carried, all you could do was circle the moon.

Then after the acceptance came a cold, cold misery. And by this you knew you really were leaving.

You knew her reason, even though she refused to speak of it. You knew that there were rules, rules of appearance that cemented bricks of hypocrisy into impenetrable walls of expectation. And though you hated yourself for it, you knew that you could not break down the walls and you knew that there would be no transcendence and there would be no redemption. All there would forever be was the cats, and she, and you, all of you, circling the moon.

All she would say as she made you promise never, ever to look for her was that it was ok, it really was, because she had already had a lifetime of looking after everyone else and just one more child wouldn't make any difference at all.

Afterwards, travelling the world didn't have the same attraction as it had done when you set out. So there was nothing for it but to go back to England and pull pints in a bar in some city noisy enough to suppress the memory of her eyes for maybe a few hours at a time. And at first you reckoned you'd not take up that place to read English at Bristol, but when the time came, with the pressure from your parents and the fact that Henry had gone to Oxford and Frank to UMIST and most of your mates were doing something similar, you didn't try to steer against the wind. As you applied yourself, at first unenthusiastically, to undergraduate courses in modern literature and the Romantic Poets, it seemed like in the voices of Keats and Shelley you could still hear the echo of her smile – but not so that it hurt, not in such a way as to tear off the scar tissue that was starting to grow over your memory. After a while you found yourself falling in love again and it was a love that would last a lifetime. But this time the love was not for a woman but for Eliot; Eliot who you liked to say was always Stearns with you but who, privately, you liked to think of as your friend Tom; Eliot who in 'East Coker' stopped you in mid-stream with words that were as beautiful as a Half Moon Bay; Eliot who finally explained it to you so that at last you understood, that 'In my beginning is my end,' and 'to arrive at where you are, to get from where you are not, you must go by a way wherein there is no ecstasy. ' And when you finally read 'Little Gidding' you knew that with Tom you had 'passed through the unknown, remembered gate, when the last of earth left to discover is that which was at the beginning.' You wept when you read those words, wondering how one man could know so much and how, though long dead, he could know so much about you; and how one woman, who like as not had never read those words, could have understood them and made the choice for you, that you were to go by a way of no ecstasy through that gate so as to discover what was at the beginning.

When undergraduate days were over and you'd surprised yourself with first class honours, and because you didn't really know what to do next, when Jamie suggested an MA in creative writing it sounded like a good way of not deciding anything at all for a bit longer. So you went, and you wrote and you were surprised to find that you could do it; that you could do it well enough that the MA led to a PhD. When you started submitting to the poetry magazines you told yourself that it wasn't really in the expectation of getting anything published. And when Poetry People took *Transcending* and called it the most enigmatic, haunting piece of writing from a new poet in years, you convinced yourself it was beginners' luck and you told no one it was about her. But when *Mirror To The Soul* won the Coleridge Prize you had to face up to your own talent. So you went on writing until you woke up one morning and found the first copies of your third collection on the doormat. And you supposed that meant that you'd finally 'arrived', whatever that meant, and that was fine, because as your old friend Tom has said, and your lover had decided for you, you had gone by a way wherein there was no ecstasy, which meant it was ok that the only thing you knew was what you did not know.

After the Englishman had gone, Harry knew Ruth was hurting badly and he knew that it fell to him to support her through her grief. He was relieved when she accepted that support gratefully. With his mother having died and his sister having left the island there was no woman in his life. Though he had no attraction to women, this was something of which, if you were wise, you did not speak openly. When running a business at Dickenson became too much for Ruth, she was more than grateful for the job Harry had arranged for her cleaning at the hotel at Half Moon Bay and she had eventually trusted him enough to tell him of the child before the rest of the world needed to know. While they were sharing confidences, Harry told her his own secret and a sense of shared conspiracy drew them still closer. Eventually, when he had proposed marriage she knew clearly what was on offer and what was not. And for this, too, she was grateful, for she had determined that in at least one way she would never belong to any man but the Englishman. This marriage would put the matter beyond question.

So with her brothers and sisters nearing the age of self-sufficiency, Ruth married Harry and named her son David. Then there was contentment and a calm, peaceful kind of happiness, restful as the lapping waves, even if this was a way of no ecstasy. As the boy grew he learned to call Harry 'Pappa.' As for Harry, his choice of pet name for David was all but inevitable. And because he had always heard his Pappa call him 'Nitro,' David never felt the need to ask for, nor did Harry feel a need to provide, any explanation.

All that is recorded of that day in 1995 is that Luis changed direction. Eleven times that season the island had been spared the coming of the hurricanes so there was no particular reason to be concerned when the meteorological offices announced that the twelfth would pass close by without making landfall. And there was no particular reason to worry when the sky turned greyer that morning, and no particular reason to fear when the rain started. But when the wind changed to an uncommon north-westerly, and that old blow Luis duly followed, when the gales started to thrash the palms and shake the hotel roof, when, as Ruth had always foretold, it was universally realised that there was no way to control the wind and that all in its path could only follow, and when Hurricane Luis concurred in her opinion and drove straight onto Half Moon Bay, taking out both the hotel and Smiling Harry's Bar, then, then there was cause for concern.

> After Luis there was the silence.
> After the silence there was denial.
> After denial there were eleven dead.
> After the deaths there was the way of no ecstasy.

You never married, of course; bought a converted barn and twenty-three acres out in Suffolk; kept your private life just that – private. Over the years you thought many times of looking for her, or sending some kind of investigator to look for her. It wouldn't have been hard on an island of 35,000 people. But she did not want to be found and you had promised not to look. So there was no investigator and no search. There was only that gnawing emptiness surging up when least expected, reminding you that you no longer possessed what once you had possessed; reminding you that now there was only the way of dispossession through an unknown, remembered gate.

When the diagnosis came through, there was no one close you could tell. You spent the remaining months as all men would – in applying yourself to doing those things that pleased you best. In your case that meant finding homes for the animals, selling the barn and setting up a trust fund for young aspirant writers from the Caribbean who wanted to study at British universities.

And as by day you settled your affairs, by night you wrote. You wrote as you had never written, with an urgency possessed exclusively by the dying. You wrote of the birth you remembered and the fables of childhood, parental abuse and the simplicity of young belief. You wrote of the mentor who had changed your writing and your life, but whom you could not name; the brother you had lost to *Desert Storm* and the OCD you had suffered silently. And you wrote of the angels and dryads and fayries and gods that ruled your world but of which you had never spoken. Then when you were done writing of your own life you wrote of the lives you did not live; the gay man you were not, the daughter you wish you had fathered. You wrote of the bureaucracy and despotism you hated and dreams of financial success and the nightmares it brings. And finally you wrote of the man you would never become; the dementia you had anticipated but outrun by dint of cancer and the death that would finally carry you over the rainbow.

Eventually all that was left was money. You bought a one way ticket to the only place where you still had unfinished business. And because there was still quite a lot of money you decided to fly Premium Economy.

So you landed at Bird, and when they opened the door you felt like the heat was going to suck you out of the plane. You hung back behind the steward's politely obstructive arm while Upper Class filed out, smug superiority written over every face. Then it was your turn to feel richer-than-thou as he stood back to let you exit, and smiled a deferential 'goodbye' while Economy stood behind him, panting for freedom. You walked down the aircraft steps into the Caribbean sunshine as the sound of the steel band wafted over the tarmac to welcome you just as it had done thirty-three years before. And because you were three or four minutes ahead of Economy you got to the taxi rank before the queue had formed. As you gave the driver your destination it made you smile to think that this time there was no one to argue with over how to split the fare.

He dropped you outside the entrance to Harmony Hall where a herd of deferential porters charged the car with the intention of carrying your bags and your computer and your golf clubs and anything else you might be about to put your hand on. You smiled at their disappointment when they saw that you came with nothing but a single holdall which you insisted on carrying yourself and you smiled even more when you saw their enthusiasm at the size of the tip you gave them for not carrying anything at all. You dumped your bag in your room, taking little notice of the view of Brown's Bay, because after Half Moon Bay nothing, even on Antigua, would ever come close to comparing. Instead you dropped down to the jetty where the hotel's little boat, Luna, was waiting to take you over to Green Island. The irony of that name was not wasted on you. On your return, for want of anything more pressing to do, you called into the art gallery to check out the Paul Elliott exhibition. Not that you were a particular admirer of his work – it was just the surname that caught your attention. So you couldn't claim any particular intervention of fate or a purposeful universe when she spoke those familiar lines to you.

She had arrived at virtually the same time as he had, having decided to come for the Elliott exhibition. She had recognised him, even though his hair was thinner and greyer than the airbrushed versions on the Internet would have her believe. When no woman exited the taxi to stand beside him, her eyebrows rose and her hopes widened. But she made no immediate move. She had no intention of positioning herself in his eyes as some overly-mature swooning groupie. He would be tired after a long flight, she reasoned, and would need time to acclimatise before she could expect from him the characteristically British response of politeness or the possibility of a more extended conversation. Later it was genuine serendipity – or, as she preferred to believe, synchronicity – that brought him into the Paul Elliott exhibition just as she was concluding her own first visit. She had been a collector of Elliott ever since she left the Caribbean, following his career more particularly when he moved to St Martin, yet had never before taken the opportunity of visiting an exhibition on home territory.

Freeborn was standing in front of a typical Elliott canvass in a clichéd evaluative pose, holding his catalogue under his right elbow as he studied the painting critically. Standing a discrete two feet from him, she mirrored his posture and matched his respiratory pace. Allowing thirty seconds or so for his unconscious sense of rapport to click in, she spoke, addressing, it seemed, the canvas, rather than the man.

"So let us sit upon the ground and weep oceans into the graves of dead children," she quoted.

He stiffened but did not turn.

She continued. "Let us rage our affronted aphorisms at the inherent injustice of the universe and the moral systems better men than us design."

He spoke. "This is a scene of peace and calm. Yet you see rage and injustice in it?"

She hesitated then answered carefully. "You and I are destined from birth to see it differently. You are English. You are a tourist. You see a cloudless sky, a warm blue sea viewed through the shutters of a colourful house. You buy the painting, take it home, hang it on the wall and tell your friends of your vacation in Antigua. I am Antiguan. I too see the sky and the sea. I see a house painted bright yellow on the outside to hide the darkness and poverty that is on the inside. I see a distant sea in which others play while I must work to feed my fatherless family."

He considered the proposition carefully. Still maintaining his posture and without turning he spoke. "You must think me shallow."

"I don't think anyone could accuse you of shallowness, Dr Freeborn – introspection, certainly, but is that not a characteristic of all writers – and of poets in particular?"

When he responded, it was not to answer the question. "Then shall we make pilgrimage to the Shrine of Incredulity…" he began.

"Adding to our number," she continued, "from the lost souls that we meet as we passed by the villages of the damned."

He turned slightly, including her in his gaze along with the seascape. "Surely it is too much to see in these houses the villages of the damned? These are pictures of joy, of hope, no?"

"True," she said, "but when you were first interviewed about that poem you insisted that the villages of the damned were habitations of the soul, not the body."

It was some moments before he responded. "Twenty-five years," he said quietly. "Twenty-five years since I built the villages of the damned."

"Yes," she answered, "but I was an intern at Poetry Life when *Transcending* was published. I remember the excitement it caused – the debates that ran over what you were really writing about."

"I've no intention of telling you now, if that's what you're here for," he replied.

"No, Dr Freeborn." She winced, knowing she had taken the conversation out of his comfort zone already. "No, I didn't mean to suggest you would change an avowed intention of a lifetime."

"You have the advantage Mrs …?"

"Dawkins, she replied, "Esther Dawkins. I'm a lifelong admirer of your work."

"Unusual," he said. "My publishers tell me I never made the impact west of the Atlantic that they would have liked. I've certainly never been recognised personally outside the UK before."

"Well, as I've said, I was an intern at Poetry Life."

"And when you returned to Antigua?"

She shook her head. "I stayed in England; married an Englishman, raised three children in Brookman's Park and worked in publishing until my husband died."

She would have caught your eye anyway, though not so much because of the way she looked as the way she moved. There was that gracefulness about her, the same elegant poise that you'd always supposed lay at the root of the ability of native peoples worldwide to carry loads on the heads. You'd often thought that whereas your people were burdened by the weight of the world on their shoulders, that same weight, differently balanced, bestowed grace and elegance upon these. And you were aware of her drawing close to you, looking at the painting next to you, then finally betraying her real purpose in that rather inelegant and over-obvious attempt to engender rapport by matching your posture and breathing. She needn't have. You had already decided to talk to her. The poetry connection came as a surprise though – that much you had to admit. Then there had been the conversation about the painting that she had viewed with eyes so different from your own, leading you to wonder if you'd had your nose so far into your own art for the last twenty-five years that you'd failed to notice everyone else's. And then there was the disclosure that reframed everything.

They had seated you at a balcony table overlooking the bay below – not that the sea was visible through the darkness of a cloud-shrouded night, though. But you could hear the breeze swaying the trees, and the lonely calls of insects hungering for species fellowship. She had talked to the waiter in some version of English that was beyond your ability to follow, ordering both food and wine that you suspected would not be available to the average tourist. The problem, of course, was that dinner held the expectation of disclosure on your part, and disclosure carried the threat of the very kind of emotional intimacy that you consistently avoided. So with little thought or no thought you did what you had long since learned protected you best in such situations. You turned the charm up to full volume, concentrated totally upon her and asked her about herself. You weren't to know the consequences.

"How did you come to leave Antigua, Mrs Dawkins?"

Her eyes glazed a little, retreating into enticing memories. "I followed a man, Mr Elliott, a white man." You did not trouble to correct her mistake. Your silence drew more from her. "It was the old, old story really. It was 1976. I was eighteen. He was twenty-one – a tourist. I met him in a nightclub at English Harbour. I fell in love. He went home at the end of his two weeks' holiday. I was miserable, so I followed him." She cradled her glass in her right hand, swirling the red wine inside, making it catch the candlelight and reflecting it onto the ceiling above the table. "It was the hardest thing I'd ever done. I knew my parents would see it as disobedience more than foolishness. They'd considered moving the whole family to London – in 1969, I think it was. Pappa'd been offered a job on the busses. Mamma had said no. And when Mamma said no Mamma meant no. It didn't matter how many years had passed or what my reasons were. They even turned down the invitation to the wedding. She wrote to me – told me I was sinning against her and Pappa and against God. 'Honour thy father and mother,' she wrote. Never spoke to me again 'til the day she died. The only contact I had with the family was through my brother."

"Is he still here on the island?"

She shifted uncomfortably in her seat. "In a manner of speaking," she replied.

Seeing her discomfort you changed subjects and the rest of the evening was given to talk of art and poetry and literary prizes. Two bottles of wine and an arrestingly good meal later, the hands of the clock drew towards the vertical. The conversation had slipped into a comfortable lull – the kind beloved of caring families and conspiratorial drinkers. After a while she saw you glance at the time and she spoke. "Crow's feet pointing to midnight, Dr Freeborn?" she asked with a knowing smile. You frowned at her, confused, until a gossamer memory wafted gently up through the layers of your consciousness.

"Now your crow's feet point to midnight..." you began uncertainly.

"when the coachmen turn to mice," She replied, raising her eyebrows.

"And the lovers yearn for freedom..."

"... when the laughter turns to ice." She smiled quizzically at you. "Surely you've not forgotten your own poem, Dr Freeborn?"

You laughed. "No," you answered, "The Jester. But I wish everyone else had! It was conceived in anger. I never should have published it."

She looked intently into your eyes. You looked back at her, gently turning down the invitation.

She had taken the unspoken rejection with excellent grace. But you were glad, nevertheless, that the words had not actually been exchanged. Shortly afterwards she had excused herself, offering a polite hope that she might see you again before your respective vacations ended. Dishonestly, you had concurred.

You slept late the next morning, hoping to avoid her at breakfast. When you did wake, you hung around the hotel for the rest of the morning and on into the afternoon, talking to no one, ignoring the view and the warm breeze that blew gently in from the hotel's main balcony. Ignoring the external environment was a habit you had developed over a lifetime. Internal stimuli, however, were a different matter.

Of course, she wasn't the first person to have confronted you with the life-wrecking reality of that unutterably foolish mistake you had made at the age of nineteen. She wasn't the first black woman you'd met who married a white man, or the first to bear mixed race children who had to live with whatever taunts and prejudices might have come their way. She was, however, the first Antiguan you'd met who had done so. And, however many times you told yourself that your mistake at such a young age was understandable, and your reaction now illogical, that fact alone still made it different. And that was what kept barging uninvited into your thoughts from the front and from behind and from the left and from the right. That was what kept beating insistently on the bark of your consciousness, like some manic woodpecker, refusing to be ignored until it broke through to gorge itself on the writhing insect nest of your silent self-deprecation. It was that incessant knocking, together with the sympathetic racing of your heart that eventually had to give voice, physical voice, until from the silence of your corner table in the bar you let out an "Oh, FUCK IT!" at the top of your voice, that stifled every conversation and turned every head in the room towards you. So you coloured up and muttered, "I'm sorry," as you rose rapidly from your table and made a hasty, tail-between-legs exit.

There was only one thing to be done, of course; only one Shrine of Incredulity for you to make pilgrimage to, and it might as well be now as at any other time. So you marched determinedly out through reception to the taxi rank and hailed the first cab without waiting for the concierge to do it for you. You had the rear door open before it stopped and you'd instructed "Half Moon Bay" before the driver had had time to ask you "Where to?" On arrival you were surprised to find just one other cab at the top of the lane leading down to the beach. You thought to yourself that Smiling Harry's Bar must, for some reason, be less popular than it had been in your day.

Steeling yourself for the potential need to summon a courteous smile should it later be required, you handed the cab driver several notes and didn't notice whether he waited or not – your thoughts were on the beach a hundred yards away. Then, making your way back into a fleeing past that was rapidly receding into the grey twilight, you fixed your face firmly towards the beach. You had intended to ignore Smiling Harry's Bar with its expected gaggle of drinkers and to go straight on down the stone steps onto the beach. You'd thought to leave your sandals at the foot of the steps, just for old times' sake. But when you got there you couldn't resist just one single glace to the left, one last look at Smiling Harry's, just for old times' sake. And one glance was all it took. She was sitting there.

She was all you saw at first, sitting at a rickety trestle table where you'd sat thirty-three years ago. The sight of her, alone, crying, was enough to exhume all your skeletons at once. So you had to turn round, you couldn't not turn round, couldn't just carry on what you were doing, pretending you hadn't seen her. And because you'd turned, you'd let it all back in, hadn't you? And that was why even though she'd not looked up, even though she'd not seen you, you had to go to her. As you started walking towards her you began to take in the rest of the scene that really was shimmering. And for just that moment you couldn't tell whether that was due to the falling light of early evening, or from the tears in your eyes or because she, and everything around her, were all ghosts. It was then you realised that she was sitting at the only complete table in the ruin of a bar that had been derelict for God knows how long.

When you reached the table, she'd still not looked up and was still crying softly.   You sat down opposite her and could have wished for a single can of beer, so cold that the condensation would have run down the side of the can, to be on the table between you. But there was no beer because there was no bar. All there was, was the silence that wrapped itself around your respective miseries. You were used to your own silence, used to your own misery. But you weren't nearly as familiar with someone else's and that made you uncomfortable. You stood it as long as you could. Then you spoke.

"What did you mean yesterday, when you said your brother was still here '*in a manner of speaking*'?"

She had known you were there as soon as you sat down, of course, but she had kept her gaze on the table, more in touch with her memories than you or the broken down bar or the evening. Finally she sniffed, wiped her eyes and looked up at you. She was silent for a while more. Then she answered – at length and surprisingly eloquently. "He was my lifeline, David, my umbilical to home. We wrote all the time. I must have asked him in every letter if there was any sign of a thaw in Mamma's attitude. There never was. She wouldn't even let me come to Papa's funeral in '82. Left word in her own will that I wasn't to be allowed to attend hers either. That was 1994. David, was I so awful? Was what I did so terrible that's she cut me off like that?"

And now she was weeping again, reaching across the table for your arm. "After our parents died Harry just told me his own news – about the bar, about his own family. He'd married the year I left. That was a surprise. I'd always assumed... well, anyway. But his son was born six months later. And if you got a girl into trouble in Antigua in 1976 you married her. No two ways about it. Harry loved that boy to bits though – sent me pictures of him all the time. Ruth christened him David – your name, but Harry always referred to his son as Nitro – said he'd be a still and quiet man, just like his father." She didn't notice that your body had stiffened. "Strange, really, that he'd refer to himself in that way. There was nothing still or quiet about Smiling Harry."

You sat there, holding her hand in the twilight, trying your damnedest to stop yourself from crushing it. You wanted to think – somehow get your head in order. But silently your mind raged its affronted aphorisms and would not be still.

"Because Mamma had died we'd planned a family reunion for '95. I was so happy I could come home at last. I was going to bring my family to meet Harry's. It was to be my first visit since

234

I'd left – nineteen years, David, nineteen years." She was weeping harder now, but desperate to carry on, to get the story out, as if doing so would somehow exorcise the pain and lay those interminably active ghosts to rest. "Then Luis came. Hurricane Luis. In 1995 Luis just… blew my people all away. I came home to see my family for the first time in nineteen years. And I did see them, David. I did see them. But they were lined up in three wooden coffins. I thought I was coming to love them and to laugh with them. But when I got here all I could do was bury them." She grabbed your hand hard and pulled it across the table to her, weeping uncontrollably onto it, shaking with great heaving sobs. You did not resist, but neither did you encourage her. All you could think of was your own twenty-five years. The twenty-five years that had passed since you built and inhabited the villages of the damned.

It was later, much later, when she had cried herself to sleep and was breathing heavily that you extricated yourself gently from her grip. Then you wandered slowly back to the stone steps and down onto the sand, not stopping to remove your sandals. As you made your way down to the water there were no more affronted aphorisms left inside you to rage. And as you made silent pilgrimage to the Shrine of Incredulity, behind you, you could hear the shuffling feet of lost souls as they added themselves to your number. Finally, you arrived at your destination, the one you had been moving towards, the one you had been returning to, for twenty-five years. There beneath the bushes, her bushes, you sat upon the ground and wept oceans into the graves of dead children.

As you sat and as you wept, the western sky threw blades of red and orange fire over the clouds. It was too dark to see much, but you could hear the night winds goading the waves into a spray that made you taste the salt on the breeze. And as you sat and as you wept, you wished, you wished so hard, for the sound of tropical waterfalls and the taste of coconut rum and the feeling of the sun on your back. And as you sat and as you wept you knew, you knew for a certainty, that somewhere out there on the dark water, their sails filled with a wind they could only follow and never control, the sea cats were circling the moon.

A note on the Author

Michael Forester is a deafened writer who divides his time between Tenerife and Hampshire's New Forest. He is 59 years old and lives with his beloved Hearing Dog, Matt. This collection of short stories has been inspired over the last fifteen years by visits to countries known and worlds unknown. Michael is the author of four previous books and has been a prize winner at the Winchester Writers' Festival. Some of his best friends are angels and dryads.

Website: michaelforester.co.uk

Email: michaelforesterauthor@gmail.com
Join Michael Forester's mailing list at michaelforester.co.uk

Thanks

I would like to express my thanks to Jacqueline Haskell and Susan Aldworth who both read early drafts of The Goblin Child and made many helpful suggestions.

My particular thanks go to my editor, Dr Stephen Carver of Green Door Designs (http://greendoordp.com) who helped me revise and professionalise the text at length. This book would not be what it is without his expertise and attentions.

Other Books by Michael Forester

Dragonsong

Rebekah, daughter of Merlin and noblewoman of Albion has been driven to madness by the murder of her lover Vidar. In her torment she bargains with the Prince of Demons to turn her into a dragon. Once transformed, she seeks to take revenge upon her father, Merlin, whom she is fooled into believing is responsible for Vidar's death.

Behind the subterfuge stands Oberon, Captain-King of Elves, who cannot foresee the devastation his jealousy and unrequited love for Rebekah will unleash upon the world of Gaia. Its salvation depends on the retrieval of the Sleep Stone from the gates of Hell. But if the stone is not returned the demon army will awake and ransack Gaia in a war that will destroy its existence. Time is the solution – but only if the gods of Asgard can find a way of stopping it.

Dragonsong is a unique epic fantasy that explores fundamental themes of good and evil, jealousy and revenge. Woven together with a gripping and powerful plot, the pattern of the language, the musicality of the form and the profound emotions invoked carry the reader to extremes of human experience and capability at both its best and worst.

Reviews of *Dragonsong*

Breakaway Reviewers: I am full of admiration for anyone who can write beautiful poetry but when they can also tell a story at the same time I find that quite remarkable.

It is about the battle between elves and men, love stories ending tragically and deceit and treachery. I would urge people to read this even if they haven't read poetry in a long time, I just found it so beautiful and the story will entrance you.

Ros Seddon: I was fascinated from start to finish. Dragonsong has everything you want in an Arthurian Legend; emotion, fear, love, war, romance and murderous plots. Good versus evil. It is the most captivating book I have read in a long time. The fact it is written in verse gives it more impact and makes it easier to digest. Michael Forester is a very talented and gifted Author and Dragonsong is written perfection.

Buy this book at michaelforester.co.uk

If It Wasn't For That Dog!

It's amazing what you can achieve with persistence, a bit of chopped liver and a second hand teddy bear…

In 2002 Michael, a deafened man from the New Forest, lost his home, his marriage, his business and his father – but he can't actually remember if it was in that order. However, in the same year someone suggested that getting a dog might be a good idea – not just any dog, but a Hearing Dog from Hearing Dogs for Deaf People. And when, in 2004, Michael was presented with a Hearing Dog of his own called Matt, he just knew life would be so much easier. Amazing how wrong you can be, isn't it!

If It Wasn't For That Dog is the story of Matt's first year with Michael, the challenges and accomplishments of climbing the Hearing Dog learning curve, the profound changes he stimulated and the inestimable joy he confers magically on everyone who

239

meets him. But most of all it is the story of the strange power of meaty treats to work miracles in doggie behaviour.

Comments about *If It Wasn't For That Dog!*

"A delightful and hugely enjoyable true life story of how an assistance dog changed a life – I loved it!" Sir Anthony Jay, writer of *Yes Minister*.

"A humorous and heartfelt chronicle about two individuals learning to dance together in perfect harmony." Dr Bruce Fogle, MBE, Vet and co-founder of Hearing Dogs for Deaf People.

Buy this book at michaelforester.co.uk